W9-BRG-781

SATAN IN GORAY

FARRAR
STRAUS
GIROUX

Books by Isaac Bashevis Singer

NOVELS

The Manor [I. The Manor II. The Estate]
The Family Moskat • The Magician of Lublin
Satan in Goray • The Slave • Enemies, A Love Story
Shosha • The Penitent • The King of the Fields
Scum • The Certificate • Meshugah

STORIES

Gimpel the Fool • A Friend of Kafka • Short Friday
The Séance • The Spinoza of Market Street • Passions
A Crown of Feathers • Old Love • The Image
The Death of Methuselah

MEMOIRS

In My Father's Court
Love and Exile

FOR CHILDREN

A Day of Pleasure • The Fools of Chelm
Mazel and Shlimazel or The Milk of a Lioness
When Shlemiel Went to Warsaw
A Tale of Three Wishes • Elijah the Slave
Joseph and Koza or The Sacrifice to the Vistula
Alone in the Wild Forest • The Wicked City
Naftali the Storyteller and His Horse, Sus
Why Noah Chose the Dove
The Power of Light
The Golem
The Topsy-Turvy Emperor of China

COLLECTIONS

The Collected Stories
Stories for Children
An Isaac Bashevis Singer Reader

S A T A N

❧ *I N* ❧

G O R A Y

Isaac Bashevis Singer
Introduction by Ruth R. Wisse
The Noonday Press
Farrar, Straus and Giroux
New York

LIBRARY OF CONGRESS CATALOG CARD NUMBER: 96-84194

I wish to express my gratitude to those who made possible the publication of this book:

Jacob Sloan brought the novel to the attention of the publisher, and undertook the difficult labor of translating a work which many considered untranslatable.

Cecil Hemley and Elaine Gottlieb worked tirelessly on it, and without their efforts this novel could never have appeared in its present form. My debt to them both is very great.

ISAAC BASHEVIS SINGER

Introduction

In 1935 the Yiddish PEN Club in Warsaw, "the highest representative of Yiddish literature in the world," determined to stimulate good writing by publishing each year the most promising first book by a local writer. To launch the series, a committee selected the novel *Satan in Goray*, which had appeared serially between January and September 1933 in the Warsaw literary monthly *Globus*. The author, Isaac Bashevis (he only assumed the family name Singer once he began to be translated into English), had been known until then for his short stories and literary criticism, and as the Yiddish translator of such European writers as Erich Maria Re-marque, Knut Hamsun, Gabriele D'Annunzio, Thomas Mann.* Under normal circumstances, this honor to a first novel should have lifted the novice to prominence. But just before the book's publication, Bashevis Singer received something far more precious than recognition from his peers—a certificate of entry to the United States of America. He left Poland for New York in April, and did not see a copy of his book until after he had reached the safer side of the globe.

Coming to America almost certainly saved Bashevis Singer's life, yet it would be many years before he regained his equilibrium as a writer. The cultural com-munity he had left behind was uniquely intense, and no one better than he had learned to turn its limitations to advantage. For the rest of his life he would continue to write fiction and memoirs about the Jewish world he had known in Poland, but of all his novels, only this one was conceived within the society that had formed him—Jewish Warsaw in what came to be known as "between the world wars." *Satan in Goray* is a distilled image of Jewish civilization in Poland at the moment before it was interrupted and destroyed. It bears unset-tling witness to a very troubled time.

---

* Also of Karin Michaelis, Stefan Zweig (his study of Romain Rolland), Moshe Smilansky (S. Yizhar). For a complete list of Bashevis Singer's translations see David Neal Miller, *Bibliography of Isaac Bashevis Singer 1924–1949* (New York: Peter Lang, 1983), pp. 233–39.

In 1918, after more than a century of partition and political subjugation, Poland reestablished its national sovereignty, but although the government was formally obliged by the Treaty of Versailles to grant cultural rights to its minorities, the new patriotic spirit turned against "the strangers within," and especially against Jews. Formally democratic, Poland was actually ruled after 1926 in semi-autocratic fashion by its military hero Marshal Jozef Pilsudski, and this ambiguous political situation had its parallel in the treatment of the Jews, who were granted formal citizenship but were faced with actual discrimination. Poland's exclusivist kind of nationalism has been described as an "ideal environment" for the development of Jewish nationalism, since it discouraged Jews from assimilating into the Polish majority, while providing them with a model of ethnic separatism.* Forcing Jews back on their own resources, Poland was also fertile ground for the development of an independent Jewish culture, for while many Jewish writers and intellectuals did try to enter Polish society at the expense of their Jewishness, the vast majority reacted to the palpable hostility by remaining within the Jewish sphere.

By the early 1930s, the 300,000 Jews of Warsaw lived in something resembling a state of siege. Anti-Semitic boycotts crippled Jewish trade; sporadic violence threat-

---

* Ezra Mendelsohn, *On Modern Jewish Politics* (New York and Oxford: Oxford University Press, 1993), pp. 37–38.

ened Jewish life; restrictive clauses blocked the entry of Jews into higher education. Emigration, once the natural route for young Jews seeking a better life, had been curtailed by America's tightened immigration policies and by worsening economic and political conditions in Palestine. Jewish Communists who tried to make the illegal crossing into the Soviet Union risked arrest by police on both sides of the closed border. Constituting over one-third of the city's population, and with ever-diminishing material prospects, the Jews of Warsaw reacted much as their ancestors had done: they concentrated on "the higher spheres," while struggling to maintain and to improve their lot as best they could.

For most young Jews after World War I, "the higher spheres" no longer meant study of Torah, of Jewish law and lore, but rather secular literature, political activism, freer self-expression. Alongside the many traditional houses of prayer and religious elementary schools, Jews established "secular" schools, and a network of competing political organizations, newspapers, theaters, and libraries. As if representing the linked spheres of modern Jewish culture, Warsaw's largest synagogue stood next door to 13 Tlomackie Street, the address of the Warsaw Association of Yiddish Writers and Journalists and of its prestigious affiliate, the PEN Club. Demobilized soldiers, young girls from Jewish towns and villages, refugees or returnees from Moscow and Berlin, anyone with literary aspirations came to this center to argue and to celebrate, as Jews had done in their houses of study. The Yiddish language was the special benefi-

ciary of Polish nationalism. Whereas immigrants to the
United States could assume that by learning English
they and their children would become Americans, the
Jews of Poland realized that their neighbors would never
accept them as Poles. Rather than try to join an un-
welcoming majority, most secular as well as religious
Jews continued to speak their own European Jewish
vernacular, even as they also spoke and read Polish and
absorbed the culture of the rest of Europe. (Isaac
Bashevis's translations of European literature were part
of a major effort to make Yiddish culture self-sufficient
by bringing into it everything—from Marx to Marinetti,
from Paul de Kock to Franz Kafka—that modern Jews
should be expected to know.)

The adjustment to Polish nationalism was never free
of humiliation. During their long history as a tolerated
minority, Jews had learned to adapt to political reversals,
but by the end of World War I expectations of citizenship
in the new republic and hopes of cultural fraternity in
a liberalized society made it harder to accept discrimi-
natory policies. The voluntary separatism of Jews as
members of a religious civilization lost its purpose once
they no longer adhered to a distinctively Jewish way of
life. As an example of this cultural predicament, modern
Jewish writers had either to forfeit aspects of their
Jewishness in order to win a place in Polish letters, or
else to go on using their native tongue inside an invol-
untary ghetto. Because the Polish PEN Club refused to
accept Yiddish writers into its ranks, Warsaw's Yiddish
writers sought and won special permission from the

International PEN Association in London to form an independent Yiddish PEN Club within Poland; Jewish writers in the Polish language had to contend with anti-Semitism as the cost of belonging to the Polish group.

Of course, Jewish anxieties were symptomatic of a universal condition. All Europe had been shaken by the Great War, its eastern sector further destabilized by the Bolshevik Revolution, the Civil War in Russia, and the bloody national struggle between Russia and Poland, from which the latter emerged unexpectedly victorious. An apocalyptic mood seized the continent, as people sought an explanation, or a portent, in so much slaughter. Many Russians and Poles found salvation in a new political order that emerged from the ruins—in the Sovietization of Russia and the national liberation of Poland. Aligned with this view, Aleksander Wat, a Warsaw–Jewish contemporary of Bashevis Singer's who became a leading figure in the post-war Polish avant-garde, spoke of the "catastrophism" of his generation, their feeling that everything had been destroyed in "an absolute earthquake." As someone fully identified with the new Poland, Wat reacted to this chasm with spiritual joy, "because here, precisely, something new could be built," something great and glorious in the wreckage!*

----

* Aleksander Wat, *My Century*, edited and translated by Richard Lourie, with a foreword by Czeslaw Milosz (Berkeley, Los Angeles, and London: University of California Press, 1988), pp. 4–5. This brilliant intellectual autobiography and Bashevis Singer's memoirs of the same time and place provide contrasting views of Jewish writers within the two linguistic communities.

Most of the Jews in these territories did not see the same opportunity for local reconstruction. Having been singled out as victims by all the warring armies alike, the Jews could not agree on any single theological or political "meaning" for their suffering. Jewish national revival gained Zionist adherents, but many religious and secular Jews could not imagine an alternative to the familiar condition of Jewish political dependency except through divine intervention or world revolution. Jews splintered into factions, each with its exclusive vision of the Jewish future, and aggression that could not be directed against the Poles (among other reasons, for fear of collective reprisal) exploded without inhibition in internecine debate.

In February 1930, a month after Isaac Bashevis had been elected the youngest member of the Yiddish PEN Club (along with Itsik Manger, Israel Rabon, and I. Papiernikov, a most distinguished cohort), the following occurred in the building: Nahum Steinberg, visiting from America, had just begun to lecture to a large audience (on the subject "Jew and Human Being"), when a gang of young Communists broke up the meeting with a barrage of rotten eggs, smashing crockery and chairs. Steinberg's credentials as a former leader of the Russian Social Revolutionary Party and minister of justice in Kerensky's provisional government, and his outspoken opposition to the Soviet regime, made him an obvious target for Communist intimidation. (Other political figures were similarly harassed, such as the Zionist Hebrew poet Uri Zvi Greenberg, who visited from Palestine.) But appeals to the authorities against such hooligan tactics would have meant informing on one's fellow Jews. Besides, the outlaw status of the Communist Party in Poland and its claim to be fighting for a better world lent its thugs a certain Robin Hood romanticism, and as long as the left opposed the fascistic right, it could claim to be championing Jewish interests. So the continental struggle for power played itself out in miniature inside the oppressively insular and politically impotent Jewish sector. The youngest inductee of PEN observed: "The spirit of politics has seized mankind as perhaps never before."*

Bashevis Singer may have been the most perfectly situated writer in this whole roiling Jewish literary community. The son of a rabbi, he had absorbed Jewish teachings before he was in a position to question them, and witnessed an array of petitioners who came to ask his father every kind of ritual and personal question. The son of a rabbi's daughter, he had spent the four years between 1917 and 1921 in his mother's native town of Bilgoraj, steeped in the customs and legends of an ancient Jewish community that was only then beginning to disintegrate. By his own admission, had he not experienced this heritage, he could not have written his first novel, which is set in the region of his maternal

---

* I. Bashevis, "Tsu der frage fun dikhtung un politik" (On Poetry and Politics), *Globus* 1: 3 (September 1932), p. 39.

ancestors, in the seventeenth-century Polish–Jewish town of Goray.

His father and mother were a study in opposites. The temperamentally sweet and trusting Pinchos Menahem Singer was so deeply immersed in kabbalistic mysteries that he prayed he might someday be granted the grace of a miracle. His wife, Batsheva, was the quintessential rationalist, who defended her belief in God the Creator through reasoned argument but remained otherwise skeptical and pragmatic. Born in the village of Leoncin in 1904, the third of four children who survived into adulthood, Isaac was brought to Warsaw when he was five, into the teeming neighborhood of Krochmalna Street, which he remembered "always full of people, and they all seemed to be shouting." Time and again in his writings the mature author re-created the scene of arrival in Warsaw, as though perpetually reliving that original moment of charged excitement. With the family's move to the capital came an escalation of friction; his brother Israel Joshua, eleven years his senior, began bringing radical atheist ideas into the home, exposing the impressionable child to all the political and philosophical challenges of the day, while his older sister Hinde (Esther) protested the fate of a traditional Jewish daughter in bitter quarrels with their mother. Long before he could understand the subtleties of the arguments, Isaac became a battleground in the struggle over modernity that was being waged in his family. These conflicts that caused the child terrible anxieties supplied the budding writer with dramatic material for a lifetime. Practically, as well as intellectually, Bashevis Singer was in luck. Israel Joshua, who had deserted from the Russian Army during World War I and joined a Jewish literary group in Kiev just after Russia's February Revolution, quickly made his mark as a writer of fiction. In 1923, back in Warsaw, he was appointed co-editor of the *Literarishe Bleter* (Literary Gazette), the most important weekly magazine that ever appeared in Yiddish, and though he did not hold this position for long, he was able to offer his younger brother a job as proofreader, introducing him to all the Jewish writers, artists, and theater people who were featured in the paper. Once Isaac began to publish his own stories, he tried to escape fraternal comparisons by assuming his mother's name Bashevis (Batsheva's). He put further distance between his own kind of modernity and his brother's social radicalism by frequenting the home of Hillel Zeitlin, the intellectual leader of Poland's modern religious Jews. At the Writers' Club, it was noticed that the two brothers never sat at the same table.* Yet, until his death in 1950, Israel Joshua remained Isaac's goad and champion. Isaac studied the craft of fiction through his brother's artistic triumphs and failures. Isaac was inoculated against Communism by his older brother's exposure to its influence. It was again Israel Joshua, brought to America as a contributor to the Yiddish daily

---

* Memoir of Z. Segalowicz, *Tlomackie 13* (Buenos Aires: Union of Polish Jews in Argentina, 1946), p. 97.

Forward, who secured for Isaac an entry visa to the United States, and later helped him land a job on this paper.

Bashevis Singer was said to be the first Yiddish writer who ever made his living exclusively through literature.* Poor as Poland was, its Jews sustained enough daily newspapers and publishing houses to provide steady work for dozens of writers and reporters, and although everything was subject to censorship, writers had greater freedom under Pilsudski than they had been granted by the tsars. After a brief attempt at writing in Hebrew, Bashevis Singer stuck to Yiddish, which at least in Poland enjoyed the strongest market among Jewish readers. Years later, in a series of novels and memoirs, he fashioned his likeness into a sexually restless "young man in search of love" who was never able to settle on a single wife or mistress. In fact, literature appears to have been his single driving passion, compared to which women were a necessary distraction. Like their father, who poured his ambition into his exegetical commentary, which he went to great lengths to have published, so, too, the three oldest Singer children were obsessed by writing of another kind; Esther eventually joined her two brothers as a writer of fiction. Right from the start,

---

* Melekh Ravitch, Secretary of the Yiddish Writers' Association, had the credentials to make this judgment: during the course of his life he published a private *Lexicon of Yiddish Writers* that came to five volumes, offering pen sketches of several hundred writers and poets whom he had known personally. Bashevis Singer shared a room with Ravitch in 1924, when he first went to Warsaw.

Isaac entered the Warsaw community of writers with supreme confidence in his own talent, and with his father's need to bring truth into a field of error.

🜚

Bashevis Singer's vantage point as a writer resembled his childhood position in the family. Having been moved around from place to place, exposed to hunger and hardship during the Great War, the boy heard two sets of explanations of the engulfing chaos, and found that he could not trust either. He lost confidence in the Omnipotent God of his parents when he saw how helpless they were in the face of crisis, but his brother's belief in a new rationally ordered society seemed, if anything, much more absurd. "There were just as many questions to be asked," he said, "of Reason as there were of God." The child was terrified by the failure of adult authority to protect him and to instruct him, and learned that he would have to fend for himself in an inexplicable universe. The characteristic narrator of Bashevis Singer's work is not the one with the answers but the one fielding the questions, poised like a referee in the middle of a playing field between the metaphysicians and the humanists, neither of whom can command the truth.

In the beginning is the child's terror, which is depicted more vividly in *Satan in Goray* than anywhere else in his fiction. The book opens at the start of the Jewish year 5426, or 1666 CE, eighteen years after the Chmelnicki massacres, which were perceived as the greatest Jewish catastrophe since the destruction of the Second Temple. In that awful time, Cossack armies rose up against Polish overlords, and fearing neither resistance nor reprisal from unarmed Jewish villagers and townsmen in their path, they overran the Jews with special brutality. Among the survivors of the fictional Jewish town of Goray in Bashevis Singer's novel are the former rich man of the town, Reb Eleazar Babad, and his only remaining child, Rechele, who becomes the book's central female figure. Born several weeks before the massacres, Rechele is taken by her mother to Lublin, and when her mother dies, she is put in the care of a widowed uncle who is a ritual slaughterer, and raised from the age of five by his aged mother. The old woman beats the child for her waywardness, and fills her mind with tales of punishing demons. When the crone dies one Yom Kippur Eve, Rechele, left alone with the corpse, experiences a paralyzing shock that leaves her partially crippled. She can never again lead a "normal" life, no more than her father can regain his position when he takes her back home to their native town.

This lonely child with the inflamed imagination bears a strong resemblance to the young boy whom Bashevis Singer describes in his autobiographical sketches:

There was one dream that repeated itself almost every night. I came to a cemetery with mounds over graves. I knew that children were buried there. Suddenly the children would emerge from under the earth. They wore little white blouses and skirts.

They played together and danced in a circle. They
also swung on swings. But they never said a word.
Were they mute? Was this the resurrection of the
dead? I recognized one little girl, Jochebed, who
had died not long after we came to Warsaw. Her
parents lived in the same building as we did and
on the same floor. I had gone out on the balcony
and saw Jochebed's funeral—a black, rectangular
hearse with compartments not unlike the phylacteries adults put on their heads and arms. The
horses were wrapped in black with holes cut out
for their huge eyes. The driver came out from our
gate carrying a black narrow box and I knew that
Jochebed was in it. He took her to a darkness of
no return. Even now, so many years later, I still see
all these visions in my dreams.*

Pious Jewish males bind tefillin, phylacteries, to their
foreheads and arms each morning, in the belief that
they are thus binding themselves to God. But the boy
in this passage who perceives the tiny black prayer box
as a hearse is no longer a candidate for religious faith.
He experiences ritual as an attempt to suffocate him,
much as Rechele's punishing "granny" tries to frighten
her into obedience. The doubt and fear that stalked
Isaac in childhood remained much realer to him than
the explanations offered to quell them. Unlike his older

---

* Isaac Bashevis Singer, *Love and Exile* (New York: Farrar, Straus
and Giroux, 1984), p. xxviii.

brother, who was a maturing adolescent by the time he was seized with doubt, Bashevis locates his crisis of disbelief in earliest childhood, before he was equipped to struggle with it as a cognitive problem. In Rechele he creates a character who has never developed any moral balance. Overwhelmed in early childhood by punishing terrors and terrorizing punishments, she never learns how to distinguish between right and wrong, and at the point of making her fateful choice of mate she is unable to protect herself from the "dead eyes" of one suitor or the ravishing lechery of another.

Rechele is the only character in this novel whose life's story is told from beginning to end. Less a heroine than the foil of events, she is born at the very moment that catastrophe befalls the Jews, and dies as a result of the even greater one that the Jews bring on themselves. This congruence of biography and national history is no accident: Bashevis Singer conceived Rechele as the child of her age. Her damaged childhood leaves her susceptible to all kinds of influences, including the promise of redemption that begins to penetrate the town of Goray when she is in her teens. Thus, when Rechele begins to transmogrify the terrors she experienced into forecasts of the approaching redemption, she cannot be blamed for having become the "voice," the vehicle, of prophetic messages. Perhaps the author means us to realize that he is also not to blame for having emerged as the "voice," or interpreter, of the demonic forces of his time.

Rechele is a study in abnormal psychology, but since

the characters in this book live two hundred years before
the birth of psychoanalysis, they experience their trau-
mas in the terminology of their time, in a vocabulary
that we would call superstition. Bashevis Singer preferred this "primitive" vocabulary to the scientific one
of his day: drawing upon a deeper level of myth, this
language better satisfies the professional storyteller, and
it points to metaphysical questions as psychoanalysis
does not. Rechele's utterances in kabbalistic language
have encouraged some readers to find in her the mystical
symbol of the Shekinah, God's immanent presence in
the midst of the people Israel, which shares the Jews'
fate in exile and suffering. But this pre-modern chron-
icler's style has a much more pungent use. Under the
protection of a twice-told tale, the author introduces
graphic descriptions of debauchery that would otherwise
have transgressed the boundaries of artistic taste and
censorship. Bashevis had to find a means of rendering
his helplessness and horror at the riot of sin that he
experienced all around him and in himself. Rechele is
described as the vehicle through which the spirit of evil
takes possession of the town, since evil must assume
some available human form in order to triumph.

   When we look into the author's artistic laboratory,
the fiction that Isaac Bashevis published prior to his first
novel, we find a story about Zisl, the daughter of a once-
prominent Jew, who moves to Warsaw upon the death
of her father and is driven to suicide by loneliness and
terror. This contemporary version of Rechele *does* visit

a doctor to try to cure her fears, but his prescribed medication induces the worst of her dreams, after which she dives through the window to her death.* Though richly descriptive, the modern story follows its heroine somnambulantly without really penetrating her inner life, except for the nightmare that precipitates Zisl's suicide. Here, the author has not yet found a way of expressing the moral and emotional waste of such a life, which to him are one and the same. By moving his subject into the past, and quickening the demonic forces that pursue his character, Bashevis Singer was able to turn Rechele into a much more disturbing and artistically compelling study in moral anxiety.

Since Bashevis Singer's interest in debauchery—not in the joys but in the perversities of sex—became the most controversial feature of his writing, this is as good a place as any to explore its function in his work. Pornography offended large segments of the Yiddish readership, including both traditional Jews, who retained strict notions of modesty, and revolutionary Jews, who subordinated all passions to politics. In later years, Bashevis Singer was accused by some of his fellow Yiddish writers of exploiting sex to gain fame among an American readership, and as the East European Jewish communities he was describing had by then been exterminated by the Nazis, he was charged with violating

---

* Isaac Bashevis, "Tsvishn vent" (Walled In), *Literarishe Bleter*, October 10, 1930, pp. 784–87.

the memory of the martyrs. These objections were expressed most sensitively by the South African Jewish writer Dan Jacobson, who wrote in 1965:

> I cannot help feeling that to some extent Singer is forced to import evil, as it were, into a world which cannot really contain or express it. The evil which obsesses him is far greater than anything his poor peddlers, ambitious rabbis, lecherous widows, grasping merchants, or their apostate sons are capable of committing . . . *They* did not gas children, burn them alive, machine gun them into pits.*

The transposition of Hitlerian evil into what had been a chaste and self-disciplined society seemed to Jacobson a breach of artistic tact. But as we see from the novel before us, Bashevis Singer had devised this vocabulary for evil a decade before the Jews of Europe were destroyed. In effect, the world of East European Jews was the only one Bashevis knew, the only raw material the author possessed and could write about with full authority. His Yiddish vocabulary, his well of imagery, his imagination and intellect were all nurtured by the same source, and he had either to "import" his sense of horror into that circumscribed sphere or not voice it at all. The rape of Rechele was his first and arguably his most effective use of this technique. Horror does not

---

* Dan Jacobson, "The Problem of Isaac Bashevis Singer," *Commentary*, February 1965, p. 51.

overtake Rechele by surprise the way it does the characters of Hitchcock movies or neo-Gothic works like *The Exorcist*, as invasions of otherwise secular rational life. Bashevis's demons are on the inside, perverting civilization as surely as the author saw it happening in every sphere of life.

In his study of Bashevis's evolution as a writer of fiction, David Roskies explains why the return to a premodern setting proved so artistically advantageous: the author was able to discard the modernist tradition he had been trying to emulate and work instead with a good plot. Instead of lyrical prose, "where you take a single piece of action and make endless variations on it, like a leitmotif in a symphony," Bashevis could tell a story to hold the reader's interest.* This literary preference satisfied a deep instinct. Bashevis Singer had been raised in a pre-modern home, and however much he educated himself in the ethics of Spinoza, he remained emotionally moored in the riven world where vying spirits of good and evil wage war over the soul. From the time he left his father's house and dropped religious practice, he transferred his spiritual interests to Jewish mysticism, the theosophy of Madame Blavatsky, the anthroposophy of Rudolf Steiner, and the many theories of telepathy and extrasensory perception that promised an unmediated encounter between

* David G. Roskies, *A Bridge of Longing: The Lost Art of Yiddish Storytelling* (Cambridge, Mass., and London: Harvard University Press, 1995), p. 278.

man and the transcendent, or at least challenged the
boundary between the natural and the supernatural.
From the beginning to the end of his career, he did
everything he could in his fiction to undermine man's
misplaced trust in his own ability. It was to Rechele that
he first consigned the worst of his torments, as if by
investing her with all his devilish doubts he hoped to
expel the terrors in his own heart.

By the time Bashevis Singer wrote his historical novel
Satan in Goray, the messianic theme had already attracted
the interest of quite a number of Jewish intellectuals
and writers. Belief in national redemption, one of the
principles of Jewish faith, runs like an electric current
through Jewish history, and the apocalyptic nature of
the First World War was bound to set off both messianic
expectations and the desire to understand them. Writers
looked for analogous moments in Jewish history, like
the aftermath of the Spanish Inquisition, when David
Reuveni (1500–35) showed up at the papal court proclaiming that he had come to restore the Jews to their
ancient kingdom, and inspired the marrano Solomon
Molcho (1500–32) to declare himself Reuveni's fellow
liberator, the Jewish messiah. Or when, according to
legend, the great Kabbalist Rabbi Judah Loew Ben
Bezalel (known as the Maharal, c. 1525–1609) created
a Golem out of clay in order to protect the Jews of
Prague from an impending pogrom. Sholem Asch,

Moishe Leib Halpern, Moyshe Kulbak, Aaron Glanz-Leyeles, H. Leivick, Aaron Zeitlin, Uri Zvi Greenberg, David Bergelson were among the Yiddish writers who composed major works on messianic and apocalyptic themes. The false messiah seemed the truest hero of the Jewish literary imagination.

Sabbetai Zevi attracted special attention; in the seventeenth century he inspired the largest and most influential messianic movement in Jewish history subsequent to the destruction of the Temple and the Bar Kokhba Revolt (events of the years 70 and 132, respectively). Gershom Scholem, the great historian of Jewish mysticism and Bashevis Singer's near-contemporary, explained how Sabbetai Zevi's vision of the cosmic redemption took such hold of the Jewish imagination that even upon his conversion to Islam in 1666—the year of the prophesied return to Jerusalem—some of his followers continued to believe in his divine mission.* Whereas Scholem charts the whole sweep of the movement that "shook the House of Israel to its very foundation," Bashevis Singer, as if looking through the opposite side of the lens, imagines the effects of Sabbatianism on a small town in Poland that is far removed

---

* In describing the kabbalistic sources of messianism, Scholem says that Polish kabbalism manifested a "unique fascination with the sphere of evil" and with demonology that finds its best expression in Bashevis Singer's stories. Gershom Scholem, *Sabbetai Sevi: The Mystical Messiah*, translated by R. J. Zwi Werblowsky (Princeton, N.J.: Princeton University Press, 1973), pp. 82–83.

from the center of action. He invites us to reexperience the original confusion of a community while the messianic outcome was still in doubt.

When the surviving Jews of Singer's novel return home after the massacres of 1648–49, they try to take up their lives as before. They seem to be fortunate in that their Rabbi Benish Ashkenazi, who has survived with half his family intact, resumes his old post with all his former authority. The distinguished descendant of generations of Goray rabbis, Rabbi Benish is as discerning about his parishioners as he is knowledgeable about the Law, but he is unable to reimpose discipline even in his own household, much less control the behavior of the town. For one thing, he is no longer confident that he understands God's will. For another, the religious discipline that sustained flourishing Goray cannot be forced back on a congregation of mourners who see no end to their suffering and no purpose to their tragedy. Travelers passing through Goray with tidings of the new messiah quickly touch off an epidemic of hope that the upright old rabbi is too weak to stop. By the end of Part One, Benish has been routed, and with his departure from Goray the believers in Sabbetai Zevi gain full control.

The forces ranged against Rabbi Benish are uncoordinated, yet cumulatively they triumph. Reb Mordecai Joseph is a religious zealot and a cripple who hates the rabbi for his superior knowledge and seizes on the new

movement as an outlet for his envy and his frustrated
dreams of power. Itche Mates the Packman is his
temperamental opposite, an ascetic so stripped of bodily
desire that he cannot consummate his marriage with
Rechele. Half deadened by fasting and self-denial, he
is regarded by the movement as already halfway to the
kingdom of heaven. For Rabbi Benish's younger son,
Levi, and his wife, Nechele, a childless couple, Sabbatianism is license to indulge in erotic excess. They
provide the salon, the alternative synagogue, for the
Sabbatian school. As for Rechele, brought up to believe
in demons and spirits, she finds her voice for the very
first time as the possessed prophetess of the new spiritual
order.

Individually, these unhappy characters are better
suited to the role of victim than of victor, but united in
the messianic faith they become an irresistible power.
The rabbi's natural heir, his oldest son, is as pathetic as
a child, and no one else among the stragglers who
returned to Goray after the great massacres shows the
least sign of taking up his authority. So once Rabbi
Benish quits the struggle, Reb Gedaliya the Slaughterer
meets with no challengers when he arrives to prepare
the Jews of Goray for the imminent messianic age.
Gedaliya's religion of joy seems to be the perfect antidote
to Benish's strict regimen. "Thou shalt" replaces rabbinic
Judaism's "Thou shalt not," as Gedaliya's ritual slaughtering allows Jews to eat meat again and his relaxation
of dietary, sexual, ritual, and legal standards invites

them to enjoy what was formerly proscribed. Although Gedaliya's kabbalistic visions presage a purified spiritual realm, he seeks pleasure for the body first, teaching that sin must be cleansed from within, through the sanctification of forbidden acts that would otherwise remain foul. In this scheme of inverted means and ends, Gedaliya considers his cohabitation with the married woman Rechele just part of the metaphysical process of turning sin into sanctity, foul into fair.

It is wondrous to behold the transformation in Goray as the town anticipates the end of the Jewish exile. The moment when Rechele bursts into prophecy is especially joyous, for it grants local Jews their own authentic miracle, an undeniable manifestation of the greater miracle to come. The rejoicing among the Jews is as extreme as the suffering that preceded it. And, for once, the balance of power appears to shift. "The gentiles who had crowded about the prayer house stepped back, terrified at the sight; they kneeled and bowed, and God's name was sanctified abroad." As the summer wears on, and a terrible drought parches the fields, the two communities react in opposite ways. The peasants turn wrathful in their hunger. But the Jews have ceased worrying about tomorrow. Neglecting their usual preparations for the winter, they dream of the golden jackets and marzipan candy that will soon be theirs for eternity.

Yet redemption can be promised only for so long before the day of reckoning finally arrives. As the novel approaches its dramatic climax, the Jews of Goray pin

all their hopes on the prophesied hour during the
Days of Awe when they will be borne on a cloud to
holy Jerusalem. The ensuing crisis dwarfs all earlier
wretchedness, even the catastrophe of the pogroms,
because there is nothing so abject as a civilization that
destroys itself. Satan triumphs when he persuades the
residents of a little town in Europe to transcend their
misery through faith in imminent redemption. The
moral collapse is so great that even after Sabbetai Zevi
ignominiously converts to Islam under threat of death
—obviously forfeiting any expectation of divine intervention—many of his followers continue to believe in
him, defying historical evidence as well as the oppro-
brium of the rabbis.

According to rabbinic Judaism, the connecting link
between the human and the divine spheres was God's
Torah, His teachings, which, once given over to Moses
and the Jewish people, were theirs alone to interpret
and to maintain. Rabbinic Judaism cultivated among the
Jews a permanent "Age of Reason," for although the
teachers believed in the revealed, supernatural source
of their codes of behavior, they considered themselves
totally autonomous, intellectually free and self-reliant
in the explication and administration of Jewish affairs.
Rabbi Benish Ashkenazi—whose patronym seems to
make him the symbolic authority for Ashkenazic Jewry,
that is, European Jews west of the Iberian peninsula—
stands firmly in this rational tradition of legal authority
and political conservatism.

Sabbatianism involved Man much more radically and dangerously in the divine plan. According to messianic legends that go back to the apocalyptic literature of the Second Temple, redemption would come, not as the result of incremental human improvements through the centuries, but on the ruins of history, which will collapse amid the "birth pangs" of the messianic age. The kabbalistic theory underlying the practices of the seventeenth-century Sabbatians taught that this material world of ours was but the outermost dark shell of God's creation. According to the mystical teachings inspired by Isaac Luria Ashkenazi of Safed (1534–72), when God projected His creative power into the world, the vessels cracked that were to have contained His divine light, spilling sparks of radiance into the darkness that is the world as we know it. Man, who contains in himself a splinter of that divine radiance, is obliged to "redeem the sparks" of holiness by battling the klippoth, the demonic powers that reside in the shadowy darkness. This was a Promethean effort in reverse, not the theft of fire from the heavens in order to benefit humankind, but the return of divine fire to the heavens in an attempt to repair the cosmic order. Although its ultimate ambition of "assisting" the Almighty is exalting in the extreme, the notion of doing battle with the forces of evil was bound to involve risky ambiguities when applied to the corporeal world. Jewish mystics had therefore tried to confine their teachings to a small elite of mature males, and opposed the use of the Kabbalah as a blueprint for political action. Not so the messianists, who undertook tikkun olam, the repair of the world, in earthly terms. Theirs is the story of *Satan in Goray.*

🐾

One of the strongest propelling forces of this novel is the narration itself. Feel, for example, the creative energy of evil in this opening paragraph:

> In the year 1648, the wicked Ukrainian hetman, Bogdan Chmelnicki, and his followers besieged the city of Zamosć but could not take it, because it was strongly fortified; the rebelling *haidamak* peasants moved on to spread havoc in Tomaszów, Bilgoraj, Kraśnik, Turbin, Frampol—and in Goray, too, the town that lay in the midst of the hills at the end of the world. They slaughtered on every hand, flayed men alive, murdered small children, violated women and afterward ripped open their bellies and sewed cats inside. Many fled to Lublin, many underwent baptism or were sold into slavery . . . The market place, to which peasants from everywhere came for the fair, was overgrown with weeds, the prayer house and the study house were filled with dung left by the horses that the soldiers had stabled there. Most of the houses had been leveled by fire. For weeks after the razing of Goray, corpses lay neglected in every street, with no one to bury them. Savage dogs tugged at dismembered limbs, and vultures and crows fed on human flesh. The hand-

ful who survived left the town and wandered away. It seemed as though Goray had been erased forever.

Bashevis Singer piles up visual images of violence, driving the prose forward as relentlessly as the Cossacks perpetrate their slaughter. The narrative is "realistic" in the way it sticks to the surface of the action, and though it adopts a moral tone ("corpses lay neglected in every street, with no one to bury them"), it subordinates the morality to descriptive detail rather than, as religious chronicles do, the action to the morality. Familiar phrases are plucked from ancient chronicles and supplemented with racier "fresh" reportage. This de-sentimentalized style became Singer's trademark. Its accumulation of detail is not confined to scenes of violence: whether he is describing the penetration of the messianic vision into Goray (Chapters 3, 5), the betrothal of Rechele and Itche Mates (Chapter 10), the storm that menaces Rabbi Benish in his final abortive attempt to control his flock (Chapter 13), or any number of moments on the way to the anticipated redemption, the author furthers his narrative through declarative sentences that produce the cumulative effect of momentum without explanation, of a natural force that is not subject to human control.

Indeed, this book could be described as a struggle between different kinds of rhetoric. Representing rabbinic civilization, the letter to Rabbi Benish that constitutes all of Chapter 13 is the stylistic antithesis to the narrator's uninflected prose. Studded with formalities, slowed by circumlocutions, inflated by hyperbole, the Hebrew epistle from the great rabbi in Lublin takes far too long to get to the point of delivering its warning about the messengers of the false messiah, and finally offers its recipient too little ammunition to stop them. The letter's information about Itche Mates is later corroborated by his behavior, but its truth remains impotent in the face of the messianists' imaginative promises. Only once the hysteria has spent its force, and most of the Sabbatians have acknowledged their error, is the language of religious discipline able to reimpose its moral certainties.

This occurs in the final two chapters of the novel, where the narrative takes the form of a tight little exemplum that has no trouble distinguishing good from bad. With this switch in rhetorical style, the author seems to be reimposing a moral order on the universe. (To heighten the effect of traditionalism, the text in the original Yiddish is arranged on these pages in the typeface and layout of seventeenth- and eighteenth-century chapbooks.) Yet, if the moral order is as certain and as plain as the final two chapters make it out to be, why were the forces of evil so persuasive in their time? Why were the characters in the novel unable to bend history as firmly as the narrator does in his summation? Far from returning us to moral certainties, this recapitulation of the narrative suggests that evil in history is well nigh unstoppable, whether it comes in the form of Cossack murderers or messianic promise. What is more, distinctions between good and evil can only be made with hindsight, retroactively, since in the heat of a historical struggle every contestant feels he is serving the cause of goodness. Readers of the concluding chapters cannot readily credit the sanctification of Reb Mordecai Joseph or the demonization of Reb Gedaliya, since these post-humous judgments distort the initial experience we had while reading the novel. If anything, the author invites us to see how relatively puny and emotionally unsatis-fying are the resources of traditional rabbinic civilization in the face of the strongest human passions. No homiletic warning against "forcing the end of history" can dislodge from the reader's experience the memory of Rabbi Benish being swept out of town in agonized defeat.

The first telling of the story does not pause to distin-guish between what is rational and what is not. Instead of dramatis personae who exercise their free will by choosing between moral alternatives, the characters in this book are driven to act or are acted upon by irrepressible impulses. Opposed to this narrative of epic simplicity* is the highly stylized moral tale of the reli-gious imagination, but in the same way that the individ-ual characters do not wrestle with their conscience, so the two forms of narrative do not creatively interact. Instead, they cancel each other out, each exposing the insufficiency of the other without possibility of com-promise.

---

* The term is Dan Miron's. See his article "Passivity and Narration: The Spell of Bashevis Singer," translated by Uriel Miron, *Judaism* 41:1 (Winter, 1992), pp. 6–17.

It is legitimate to wonder where the novelist stands in this conflict between remorseless idealism and re-straining human discipline. Bashevis told his Yiddish readers how he saw himself:

> My brother freed himself from revolutionary phraseology, but he continued to believe, or rather to hope, that the human species would come to its senses. He still believed in so-called progress. Little by little, humankind would learn from its mistakes. My brother needed this faith in moral progress, although the facts refuted him left and right. In a sense, I had taken over the role of our parents: in our conversations I mercilessly destroyed his hu-manistic illusions. Now I regret it, because with what could I replace them? At least my parents preached religion. I had nothing but the power to destroy.*

Bashevis never believed with the humanists and so-cialists that rational beings could work with increased mutual understanding toward the progressive improve-ment of their species. He did not accept Hegel's view of ameliorative history, and saw no middle ground between disciplining religion and wanton license: either/or; either Rabbi Benish or Reb Gedaliya, and the one could only rule by expelling the other. He was not a

* Isaac Bashevis, "A por verter vegn zikh" (A Few Words About Myself), *Svive* (May 1962), p. 17.

AMELIORATIVE HISTORY
TO MAKE BETTER OR TO
MORE TOLERABLE — TO
GROW BETTER — IMPROVE

moral relativist, insisting as his parents had done on the
absolute distinction between good and evil, and on the
ontological reality of good and evil in the universe. But
neither did he believe that religious discipline could
withstand any longer the inspired assaults against it. He
did not think that what was necessary was possible. In
this, his first full-length novel, written when the messianic forces of Europe were sweeping away all reasoned
opposition like so much chaff in the wind, Bashevis
shows the fatal triumph of the revolutionary impulse
that can never be stopped in time. The author's reim-
position of tight moral strictures at the conclusion of
his book only draws attention to its futility.

In the preface to the 1935 edition of *Satan in Goray*,
the Yiddish poet Aaron Zeitlin, a close friend of both
the brothers Singer, tells us what his contemporaries
found to admire in the book. He calls the novel an epic
poem, and compares its prose rhythm to a musical
composition. He marvels at the author's descriptive
powers, quoting many passages of deft and economical
characterization. He says that "through some chemical
secret" the book fuses lyrical, narrative, and dramatic
elements into a work so concentrated that not a word
could be added or sacrificed without damage to the
whole. The ethnographic impulse had always been
strong in Yiddish literature, which sprouted at precisely
that moment in the late nineteenth century when the
Jewish way of life was undergoing convulsive change.
This novel goes far beyond any predecessor in its
compression of various types of folklore and historical

information. It is written as densely as though Bashevis thought it was the last book he would ever write. As Zeitlin observes, there is hardly another modern Yiddish novel that can compare with it in the richness of its diction or the crispness of its style.

Only at the end of his preface does Zeitlin admit the controversial contemporary aspect of the book: "In today's Yiddish literature, which faithfully submits to the harness of proletarian 'requirements,' works like Bashevis's are *a splendid anachronism* [emphasis in the original]."* In other words, the most striking feature of *Satan in Goray* was the way it defied the political correctness of its day, the prevailing ideological insistence that literature further the socialist cause. Zeitlin thought the novel subverted political propagandists by recalling the language and atmosphere of a religious past.

It is by now commonplace to recognize that every historical novel is also the product of its own time, whether or not the author is consciously manipulating his material to address a contemporary issue. Just below the surface of this seemingly antiquated story about the followers of Sabbetai Zevi throbs the messianic hysteria that Marxism generated in the ruins of Eastern Europe following World War I and that continued to dominate Jewish intellectual circles in the 1930s, just as Zeitlin says. Bashevis's friends who warned against Communism

---

* Aaron Zeitlin, "Fun di aroysgeber" (From the Publishers), foreword to *Der sotn in goray* (Warsaw: Yiddish Pen Club, 1935). Zeitlin deleted this single final sentence of his preface from the two subsequent Yiddish editions of the book (New York, 1943, and Jerusalem, 1972).

were treated like those skeptics in the novel who try to warn against Sabbetai Zevi. But more than the tactics of any one political group, the book exposes the phenomenon of "applied messianism" that devours the very hopes it feeds upon.

Satan in Goray is not a political parable in the strict sense of the word, not like George Orwell's *1984* or *Animal Farm*. Orwell's fiction drew political parallels between Big Brother and Joseph Stalin, between Communism's version of equality and the pigs' exegetical codicil that "some are more equal than others." And because Orwell's satire was so true, these books have been somewhat dated by subsequent changes in Russia that culminated in the fall of the Soviet Union. Even more passé is Sinclair Lewis's best-selling novel of 1935, *It Can't Happen Here*, which projects a Nazi-style political evolution within the United States. By contrast, Bashevis Singer's "story of long ago" evokes the atmosphere of political hysteria without any contemporary allusion whatsoever. A pure tapestry of ethnographic and historical threads, the novel will recall the 1930s only to those who already know something about the political climate between the two world wars, or who are prompted to look for correspondences. But, for such readers, this "splendid anachronism" may loom as one of the finest political novels in the Western canon. Evil is never so powerful as when it claims to be redemptive; redemption is never so persuasive as when it follows great suffering; no suffering will compare with the consequence of "forcing the end" of history. The Jews' experience with failed messianism becomes a parable for all such revolutionary ecstasies.

♈

After reading this novel, the reader might be interested to know how the author fared in America, and how this early masterpiece figures in the body of his work. On the whole, Singer continued to have the most fortunate career in modern Yiddish letters. Almost from the moment he arrived in New York, he became a regular contributor to the *Forward*, the oldest and most widely read Yiddish daily in the world, which offered Yiddish writers the only moderately secure job in their profession. He was a prolific contributor to the paper, publishing first under the name Isaac Bashevis, then from 1939 as Y. Warshavski, and from 1942 as both Warshavski and D. Segal, reserving "Bashevis" for stories that he published in the better Yiddish journals in New York and Tel Aviv.* Despite an initial effort to distinguish the type of writing he did under each of these pen names, he wrote some of his finest memoirs as the "journalistic" Warshavski, and some fairly sloppy novels under his "literary" name Bashevis.

The talent of this writer was never in doubt. At age twenty-one he won a prize, in a Warsaw competition, for his first published story, and at twenty-nine he wrote

---

* David Neal Miller describes the work written under these pseudonymns in *Fear of Fiction: Narrative Strategies in the Works of Isaac Bashevis Singer* (Albany: SUNY University Press, 1985).

Satan in Goray. The American literary critic Irving Howe
liked to recall the "transforming moment" when he first
discovered Bashevis Singer. He had been working with
the Yiddish poet Eliezer Greenberg on a major anthol-
ogy of Yiddish stories, and upon hearing "Gimpel the
Fool" read aloud to him in Yiddish, he was overcome
with excitement: "how often does a critic encounter a
major new writer?"* Translated by Saul Bellow and
published in *Partisan Review* in 1953, "Gimpel the Fool"
sparked an intense interest in Singer that continues to
the present day. Previously, Sholem Asch (1880–1957)
had been the only Yiddish writer to become an American
best-seller, but Asch's sprawling novels had never im-
pressed the serious critics. By contrast, Singer appealed
alike to the editors of *Commentary* and *Playboy*, and he
has been translated into twenty-nine languages. In 1978
he became the first Yiddish writer to win the Nobel
Prize in Literature.

　　Nevertheless, Singer's transition from Warsaw to New
York, like the later transposition of his works from
Yiddish to English, had an ambiguous effect on his
career. We know how very cramped the author had felt
in Jewish Warsaw. Indeed, Bashevis had contributed his
share to what he called the "demoralization and hysteria"
of Warsaw's Yiddish literary community in blistering
attacks on his fellow writers.† He had attacked, first, the

---

* Irving Howe, *A Margin of Hope: An Intellectual Biography* (San Diego,
New York, and London: Harcourt Brace Jovanovich, 1982), p. 262.
† B-s, "Di shraybers un di zidlers" (The Writers and the Slanderers),
Globus 15 (September 1933), p. 84.

careless editorial supervision of the newspapers where writers churned out their serial novels without any pressure to improve; second, the symbolism and modernism that simply indulged the writer's sloppiness: instead of sustaining dramatic tension, the modernists often neglected the human subject which was the mainstay of fiction; third, the ideological tendentiousness that subordinated character and action to political ends. It was largely in reaction to this perceived "undisciplined" Jewish cultural atmosphere that Bashevis Singer developed his own spare style.

But once he quit the claustrophobic, madly contentious Yiddish literary community, he was faced with the opposite problem. America rewarded individual initiative and beckoned immigrants away from their cloistered cultures, but the consequence of greater freedom and economic opportunity was a relaxation of collective consciousness, including evaporation of the Yiddish language. Here the Association of American Yiddish Writers had only a paper address, and none of its members seemed to know or to care very much about him. In Warsaw he had labored like Heracles to clean out the Augean stables, but in New York he fell prey to demoralization. This period of his life he was later to characterize as "lost in America." He began to produce for the Yiddish daily *Forward* just the sort of careless writing he had targeted for criticism only a short time before.

For example, several months after landing in New York, Bashevis Singer began serializing in the *Forward* a novel about Jacob Frank, who proclaimed himself the Polish reincarnation of Sabbetai Zevi, and in this messianic crusade led thousands of his followers into the Catholic Church. Frank's heretical practices far exceeded those of the Sabbatians, and this time Bashevis highlighted the kind of dramatic and erotic adventures that he had curbed in *Satan in Goray*. Bashevis already knew that because sex had much greater shock value within a puritanical setting than in a relatively promiscuous modern context, the confinement of a work of fiction to the Yiddish sphere of Eastern Europe could help stimulate prurient interest. Here he capitalized on that interest. The editor of the *Forward*, Abraham Cahan, must have had some misgivings about serializing *The Sinful Messiah*, as can be seen from his explanation to the readers that its racy descriptions of orgies and intrigues were truly the stuff of Jewish history, and that the author Bashevis Singer, having studied and read "almost everything there was to find" about this wild sect, could be trusted to distinguish between the truth and inane fantasy.* But the author was well aware of the difference between the controlled novel he had just

---

* Abraham Cahan, "Jacob Frank," *Forward*, October 5, 1935, p. 12. Incidentally, nowhere in this introduction does Cahan mention the recently published *Satan in Goray*, either because Singer had not brought it to his attention or because Cahan did not want to publicize any precedent. This is indicative of the great cultural distance between Warsaw and New York, despite personal contacts between some individual writers. The Yiddish literary circles in Poland tried to keep up with their counterparts in America, but there was much less intellectual traffic in the other direction.

published in Poland (in a small magazine whose editors had to sustain most of its costs) and this melodramatic self-imitation. He never put out the Jacob Frank novel in book form and, in despair over his writing, published no fiction for seven years. In 1943 he reissued *Satan in Goray* in a volume that contained only five additional shorter works, each one thematically related to the novel, and all brilliantly crafted.

Bashevis sensed that at the *Forward* and in the American marketplace no one but he might ever know or care whether he was exploiting the shock value of such themes as "the sinful messiah" or harnessing erotic energy to a work of art. What is more, once the Germans captured Warsaw in September 1939 and imposed a reign of evil that defied human imagining, Bashevis saw his family and the world he had known disappear in its entirety, along with its standards and restraints. It was during the war that Bashevis first began to adopt the persona of a playful demon, corresponding to the author who could defile the historical reality of Polish Jewry at will. He had always feared the corruption of human behavior once people perceived that there was no one left to care. In America, he felt he was writing in a moral vacuum.

As I have said, the talent of Isaac Bashevis Singer has never been in doubt. The argument over his work will revolve, rather, over the relative merit of the various genres in which he wrote, and over the quality of the works within each genre. In awarding Bashevis Singer the Nobel Prize in Literature, the Committee cited *In*

My Father's Court, the first of Bashevis's autobiographical collections that were brought out in English. The memoiristic genre, which makes the greatest claims for "truth," was also favored by Yiddish readers of the daily press. Three additional books of memoirs were collected in *Love and Exile*, and there are several volumes more among the columns that Singer wrote for the *Forward*. His strong attraction to the autobiographical genre is also evident in such novels as *Shosha* (1978), *Enemies, A Love Story* (1972), *Meshugah* (1994), *The Certificate* (1992), *Scum* (1991), whose protagonist Aaron Greidinger bears a striking resemblance to what we know about Isaac Bashevis Singer from his memoirs,* and *Shadows on the Hudson* (1997).

Many critics believe that Bashevis Singer's true genius lies in the short story, a claim one can confidently make for Yiddish literature as a whole. Some of his very best stories are written in the first person, with the devil as narrator. In his later years, Singer began writing stories for children; in addition to the commercial enticements of this lucrative market, the "simple narrative" appealed to him as an antidote to the hyper-sophistication of so much modern culture.

Since few of Singer's literary essays and reviews have been translated, the English-language reader may not suspect how acute and acerbic were his literary judg-

---

* Khone Shmeruk was the first to investigate correspondences between Singer's memoirs and these autobiographical novels, in "Bashevis Singer—In Search of His Autobiography," *The Jewish Quarterly* 29: 4 (Winter, 1981/2), pp. 28–36.

ments. Before American audiences the author liked to cast himself as a puckish character, parrying serious questions about the future of Yiddish with references to the ghosts who would go on speaking the language into eternity, and to the army of graduate students that would someday comb Yiddish literature for thesis topics. But he had thought hard about the special conditions of Yiddish fiction, and particularly in his early years, he used review essays as a testing ground for his own ideas about his craft.

The novel was his greatest challenge. With the exception of *Satan in Goray*, all of Bashevis Singer's novels in book form were serialized in the *Forward*, then revised for publication either in Yiddish or in English. In addition to the autobiographical novels listed above, these include *The Family Moskat* (1950), *The Magician of Lublin* (1960), *The Slave* (1962), *The Manor* (1967) and *The Estate* (1968), *The Penitent* (1983), and *The King of the Fields* (1988). Revising his novels with the benefit of English-language editors, Bashevis had an opportunity to tighten their structure, and knowing that these English-language editions rather than the original Yiddish ones would form the basis of translation into other languages, he paid close attention to their alteration. He encouraged his translators to eliminate some of the semantic or cultural references that would have been foreign to modern and non-Jewish readers, realizing with his powerful artistic instincts that the very kinds of details that would awaken sharpest associations in Yiddish would fall flat outside it. Evaluation of these works will remain complicated by considerations of cultural context, precisely because of the care the author and his editors took in transposing these works from one culture to another.

In this sense, *Satan in Goray* remains unique among Bashevis Singer's novels. It was originally written for an elite readership, and cast under tremendous creative pressure in a tight narrative mold. Twice republished in Yiddish, it was translated into English with no apparent help from the author, scrupulously deferent to the original. For such reasons, readers may find this to be the most difficult of Bashevis Singer's novels. They may also conclude with me that it is his very best.

Ruth R. Wisse
Harvard University
1996

PART ONE

❦ 1 ❦

The Year 1648 in Goray

In the year 1648, the wicked Ukrainian hetman, Bog-
dan Chmelnicki, and his followers besieged the city
of Zamosć but could not take it, because it was
strongly fortified; the rebelling *haidamak* peasants
moved on to spread havoc in Tomaszów, Bilgoraj,
Kraśnik, Turbin, Frampol—and in Goray, too, the
town that lay in the midst of the hills at the end of the
world. They slaughtered on every hand, flayed men
alive, murdered small children, violated women and
afterward ripped open their bellies and sewed cats
inside. Many fled to Lublin, many underwent bap-

tism or were sold into slavery. Goray, which once had
been known for its scholars and men of accomplish-
ment, was completely deserted. The market place, to
which peasants from everywhere came for the fair,
was overgrown with weeds, the prayer house and the
study house were filled with dung left by the horses
that the soldiers had stabled there. Most of the houses
had been leveled by fire. For weeks after the razing
of Goray, corpses lay neglected in every street, with
no one to bury them. Savage dogs tugged at dismembered limbs, and vultures and crows fed on human
flesh. The handful who survived left the town and
wandered away. It seemed as though Goray had been
erased forever.

Only years later did its destitute citizens begin to
return, a handful from each large family. Meanwhile,
those who had been young men when Goray was dev-
astated had turned gray, those who had been a power
in the community were now clad in sackcloth and
brought only beggars' bags with them. Some had left
the path of righteousness, others had fallen into melancholy. But it is the way of the world that in time
everything reverts to what it has been. Shops which
had long stood closed behind rusted shutters opened
one by one; bones were borne away to the untended
cemetery, where they were all buried in one common
grave; the flaps of booths were timidly lowered; apprentices mended the damaged roofs, repaired the
chimneys, and painted over blood-and-marrow-splat-
tered walls. With long poles, boys fished for human

bones in dried-up streams. Gradually, the runners began to move again from village to village, buying corn, wheat, greens, and flax. The peasants in the surrounding villages had been too terrified even to set foot in Goray for fear of the demons whose dominion it was. Now they rode into town again to buy salt and candles, material for women's smocks and blouses, cotton kaftans and clay pots, and all kinds of necklaces and ornaments. Goray had always been isolated from the world. Hills and dense woods extended for miles about the town. Winters, the paths were the lurking-place of bears, wolves, and boars. Since the great slaughter the number of wild beasts had multiplied.

Last of its citizens to return to Goray were the old rabbi, the renowned Rabbi Benish Ashkenazi, and Reb Eleazar Babad, formerly the richest man in the community and its leader. Rabbi Benish brought more than half of his family with him. He moved immediately into his old house, near the prayer house, began to supervise the observance of the laws of ritual diet, saw to it that the women went to the ritual bathhouse at the proper time, and that young men studied the Torah. The rabbi had left two daughters and five grandchildren behind in the cemetery at Lublin. He had lived in exile all these years, but misfortune had not changed his ways. He rose early, studied the Talmud and its commentaries by the light of a waxen candle, immersed himself in cold water, and recited prayers in the synagogue at sunrise. Rabbi Benish was in his sixties, but his skin was still smooth, he had lost none of his white hair, and his teeth had not fallen out. When he crossed the threshold of the prayer house for the first time after many years—tall, big-boned, with a full, round, curly beard, his satin coat reaching to the ground, the sable hat pulled down over his neck—all those sitting there rose and pronounced the blessing in thanks to Him who revives the dead. For there had been reports that Rabbi Benish had perished in Lublin during the massacres on the eve of the Festival of Tabernacles in the year 1655. The fringes of the vest that Rabbi Benish wore between his shirt and coat tumbled around his ankles. He wore short white trousers, white stockings, and half-shoes. Rabbi Benish grasped between his index finger and thumb the thick eyebrow that hung over his right eye, lifted it the better to see, cast a glance at the darkened, peeling walls of the prayer house and its empty book chests, and loudly declared: "Enough! . . . It is the will of our blessed God that we begin anew."

Rabbi Benish Ashkenazi had inherited his office in Goray from generations of rabbis. He was an author of commentaries and responsa, a member of the court of the Council of the Four Lands, and was reckoned among the most brilliant men of the day. In former times many deserted wives had made the long trip to out-of-the-way Goray to receive permission from Rabbi Benish to remarry—for with all his learning and brilliance, Rabbi Benish was one of those who construed the Law liberally. Often emissaries had come to Goray from famous communities in an attempt to persuade him to accept coveted rabbinical posts—but all went away disappointed. Rabbi Benish wished to end his days in the place where he had inherited his office. And now he was home again. Miraculously, there had been little damage to his house. The two oaken book chests, once more filled with folios and manuscripts, stood where they had previously, along with the old-fashioned chairs covered in yellow satin, and the copper candelabra hanging down from the ceiling. Sacred volumes and writings were piled an ell deep in the attic. It was even rumored that somewhere in the house a clay man was hidden, a Golem that had once helped the Jews of that town in a time of persecution.

Reb Eleazar Babad returned to Goray with only one daughter. The older daughter, the married one, had first been raped by the Cossacks and then impaled on a spear. His wife had died in an epidemic; Reb Eleazar's only son had disappeared, and no one knew what had happened to him. Since the first floor of his house had been wrecked, he moved into an attic room. In the old days Reb Eleazar had been famous for his wealth. He had dressed in silk even on weekdays. It had been the custom for a bride to be led to his house, where the wedding band would play in his honor. In the prayer house the cantor would wait for Reb Eleazar before reciting the Eighteen Benedictions, and on the Sabbath his household and the holiday guests dined at a table set with silver. Many a time the lord of Goray drove up to Reb Eleazar's in his carriage to pawn his lady's jewelry for gold ducats.

But Reb Eleazar was now unrecognizable. The long, narrow body had bent like a candle, the wedge-shaped beard had turned ash-gray, the emaciated face was brick-red. Reb Eleazar's eyes, set close to his bony, peeling nose, now protruded, and seemed always to be looking for something on the ground. He wandered about wearing an old sheepskin hat and nondescript housecoat; a rope girdled his waist, his feet were wrapped in rags, like those of beggars. He never came to the prayer house to pray; he did his own housework, sweeping up, preparing food for himself and his daughter, and even going to the market to fetch a copper's worth of food from the women who sat near their carts. Whenever he was asked how he was getting along and how he had fared during the time he had been away, Reb Eleazar would shiver as though at some dreadful thought, would shrink into himself, look past his questioner's shoulder, and reply, "Why talk about it? What's the use?"

Some said he was doing penance for his sins. Teme Rachel, the pious woman, added that once late at night she had passed his window and had observed him pacing back and forth and speaking aloud in a sad voice. Others whispered that he was out of his mind, that he did not take his clothes off when he went to sleep, and that he placed a long knife under

his pillow nights, like a woman in labor, to keep
away the devil.

His daughter, Rechele, who was seventeen years
old, had a lame left foot and seldom showed herself
outside, preferring to remain hidden in her room.
She was tall, with a greenish complexion, but handsome, with long black hair that hung down to her
waist. In the early days after Reb Eleazar's arrival
people had tried to arrange a match for her, because
it was a pity for so old a girl to sit at home without a
man. But Reb Eleazar did not answer the match-
makers, never said either yes or no, and they soon
grew tired of useless talk. Besides, Rechele's behavior
was strange from the beginning. When it thundered
she would scream and hide under the bed. To the
young wives and girls who came to call on her she
said nothing, driving them away with her indifference.
From early morning till night she sat alone, knitting
stockings or merely reading in the Hebrew volumes
she had brought from abroad. Sometimes she would
stand at the window braiding her hair. Her large,
dark eyes gazed beyond the rooftops—wide-open, brilliant, as though seeing things concealed from others.
Though Rechele had a deformity, she aroused sinful
thoughts in men. Women shook their heads when
they spoke of her, whispering:

"The poor lonely orphan . . . so feeble a child.
And such a melancholy thing."

❦ 2 ❦

Rabbi Benish and His Household

In Lublin Rabbi Benish had been constantly busy. The events of 1648 and 1649 had left thousands of women neither married nor widowed, since it was uncertain whether their husbands were alive. Often the rabbinical court had to veer from the strict letter of the law and release a woman from the marriage bond. In the anterooms of the community house where Rabbi Benish sat in judgment with other great rabbis, there was always a crowd of weeping women. Some of these unfortunates wandered from town to town, searching the registers of the holy burial socie-

ties for the names of their lost husbands. Others,
forced to release their brothers-in-law from the obli-
gation of marrying them, complained bitterly of the
fee demanded for such consent. Often, one of these
women would remarry, only to have her first husband
return; he would have escaped from Tartar slavery
or been ransomed by the Jewish community of Stamboul. Around the building where the Council of the
Four Lands met, marriage brokers bustled, matching
prospective couples and extracting advances on their
fees; beggars tugged at the jackets of passers-by;
persons who were half- or completely mad laughed,
cried, sang; children who had lost father and mother
wandered about the courtyard, abandoned and
mangy, insolently begging. Daily, emissaries arrived,
each from a different Jewish community, recounting
the suffering that had come on the heels of Chmelnicki and the Swedish soldiers. More than once Rabbi
Benish begged God to transport him from this world,
as he no longer had the strength to hear these sorrowful stories.

But here in Goray all was calm. There were no
judicial disputes, few queries concerning the holy
law. True, the town offered him only a scant living,
but for that very reason the rabbi had enough time
for himself. His room was separated from the rest of
the house by a large corridor, and silence reigned
throughout. A solitary fly buzzed, beating against the
windowpane; a mouse scratched along the floor; the
cricket behind the stove would chirp monotonously

for a few minutes, then listen to its echo for a long while before beginning anew, as though mourning an unforgettable sorrow. The ceiling was blackened by smoke; the walls were mildewed, and the stain of a white-and-green mold would appear nightly, rising, it seemed, from another world. On the table lay unlined sheets of paper and goose-feather quills. Rabbi Benish sat there for hours at a time, deep in thought, his high forehead wrinkled, and every now and then he would cast an expectant glance at the yellowed window curtains. Although more than half the town had returned by now and found shelter, the sound of talk and of children at play was rarely heard outside. It seemed as though the few Jews who had come back to Goray were all indoors, their ears alerted for news of the enemy's vengeful return.

Rabbi Benish knew his people. Although constantly preoccupied with profound meditation, he kept everyone in mind, even calling women by name. When Rabbi Benish arrived in Goray it was summertime, a busy season. The townspeople were hauling timber from the forest; saws screeched and hammers banged, and children ran about. Young girls came out of the woods carrying full pails of blueberries and wild strawberries, heavy bundles of branches, baskets of mushrooms. The lord of Goray allowed the townspeople to fish in his pond, and every family dried fruit to preserve it for the rest of the year. At dusk, when Rabbi Benish walked to the prayer house, the air smelled of fresh milk and of chimney smoke, and everything seemed to be as it had been before. At such moments, he would raise his eyes to Heaven and thank God for having saved a remnant of his flock, for not having allowed it to be completely destroyed, as they had been in other communities.

But now, after the Feast of Tabernacles had passed, as the cold season began, the havoc in Goray became more apparent. Most of the empty windows were boarded up or stuffed with rags. There were no warm clothes for the children to wear, so they sat at home and did not attend school. The rain left pools of water to mirror the houses with their patched walls and roofs. The harvest was meager, and the little wheat that was reaped could not be milled, for the miller was one of those who had perished. The mill locks had been broken, the earthen dam trampled. For a bit of bread the folk of Goray had to crush the kernels by hand in oaken bowls and bake the heavy dough over an open flame. Many families never had a taste of even this poor bread.

To make matters worse, Rabbi Benish's household was engaged in an interminable family quarrel that had been smoldering for years, since before 1648.

The rabbi's eldest son, Ozer, was a worthless man, a bad scholar and an idler. Almost fifty years old, he still sat at his father's board with his wife and children. Ozer was tall, stooped, rapid in his movements, and quick-tempered. His rumpled velvet hat was always askew, his shirt open, his vest unbuttoned and stained. He had a nose that curved like a beak, two large bird eyes, and a straw-colored, unkempt beard. Before 1648 Ozer used to sit in the tavern for days on end, playing chess or gambling with dice, enjoying all kinds of gossip and malicious talk. He never thought of his wife and children, had no serious ambition, and always held a piece of chalk between his fingers with which he perpetually marked calculations on every closet and table that he passed. He was the same scatterbrain now as before 1648. The rabbi disliked Ozer, and seldom spoke a word to him. Ozer sat in the kitchen with the women, warmed himself at the stove and peered into the pots, until his mother, the rabbi's wife, would drive him away with a broom, crying, "Aren't you ashamed, a man your age! Why, it's a public scandal!"

Levi, the rabbi's youngest, was in his thirties, and quite different from his brother. He was short, black as a gypsy, immaculate, a haughty man with a dignified bearing. His roundish beard was fine-combed, his earlocks genteel and curled. Levi brought fine garments back with him from Lublin, and strolled around shabby Goray in a flowered silk dressing gown with satin trim, slippers with pompons, and a sparkling new velvet hat on his head. His gait was measured, he mingled little with the other members of the household, and rarely entered his father's room. His mother sent delicacies to him in his alcove, stuffing and pampering him until she aroused the envy of Ozer and his children. Moreover, Levi's wife Nechele had been the only daughter of a rich merchant. Her

father had been murdered in Narol during the massacre in that town; Nechele had been reared in the
home of wealthy relatives in Lublin. She behaved as
she had in the past, lying abed till late in the afternoon waiting for her mother-in-law to send the maid
to her with a jug of milk. Nechele even reckoned her
barrenness a virtue. Weekdays she wore silk headkerchiefs and gold earrings. Her lean fingers were clut-
tered with rings. Thin, flat-chested, with an aristo-
cratic figure, unhealthily red cheeks, and eyes weak
from crying, Nechele never ceased complaining of
how she had fallen into a vulgar house; her thin lips
mumbled constantly, and her nose crinkled as though
she suffered from the nasty Goray smells. She decorated lavishly the room given to her and her husband.
The walls were hung with various canvasses: repre-
sentations of *The Sacrifice of Isaac, Moses Holding
the Tables of the Law, The High Priest Aaron in
Breast-Plate and Vest*. The bed was strewn with
small pillows. A thick embroidered curtain hung over
the windows, keeping the conjugal chamber in semi-
darkness. Nechele, lady-like in an embroidered
blouse, a feather duster in hand, sought out dust and
cobwebs, and addressed her husband with melancholy sighs that kept alive the fire of discontent.

Ozer's wife and children, on the other hand,
dressed in crude clothing, lived in crowded quarters,
and ate in the large kitchen with the servant girl. In
addition to them, Rabbi Benish's household included
several orphans left behind by his daughters who had

died in Lublin during the cholera, and one daughter who had been divorced. All these individuals conducted a silent campaign against Levi and his wife, transferring their resentment to the rabbi's wife, who they considered had succumbed to Levi. The various parties also were at one another's throats, and told stories behind one another's backs, the following being adversaries: Nechele and the rabbi's wife; Nechele and her sister-in-law; the two brothers; the orphans and their grandmother. Of Nechele it was said that she had bewitched her husband, causing him to remain in love with her and follow her false ways. Ozer's wife swore that Nechele went out to gather herbs every Sabbath eve. Someone also once met her going in to see the witch, Kunnigunde, who lived beyond the town, near the gentile cemetery.

In the past, Rabbi Benish had tried to bring peace to his household. The rabbi feared the sin of controversy, knowing that every visitation inflicted on a house sprang from this transgression. But now the old rabbi no longer had the strength to make peace. His years were numbered and there was much to put in order. He had several works to complete. Moreover, the bitter persecutions of the years 1648 and 1649 had re-awakened in him the old paradoxes regarding faith, predestination and freedom of will, and the suffering of the virtuous. Rabbi Benish sat alone, locked in, and no longer visited his wife Friday nights in her bedroom. On the rare occasions when a member of his family came into his room to begin tattling and informing, Rabbi Benish would rise to his full height; his beard leaping like a living thing, one hand beating on the oaken table, the other pointing to the door.

"Get—out!" he would shout. "I've heard enough. Pests!"

✿ 3 ✿

Extraordinary Rumors

For a number of years now, extraordinary rumors had swept through Poland.

During the time Rabbi Benish still dwelt in Lublin he had heard amazing things. All men were discussing the Jerusalemite rabbinical emissary, Baruch Gad, who, in journeying through a desert, had blundered across the other side of the river Sambation; he had brought back with him a parchment letter from the Ten Lost Tribes, supposedly written by the Jewish king, Achitov, the son of Azariah. According to this letter, the end of days was near. Copies of the writ were in the hands of a few Land of Israel Jews who journeyed from country to country collecting money.

The greatest cabalists in Poland and other lands uncovered numerous allusions in the Zohar and in antique cabalistic volumes proving that the days of the Exile were numbered. Chmelnicki's massacres were the birth-pangs of the Messiah. According to a secret formula, these pangs were destined to begin in the year 1648 and extend till the end of the present year, when the full and perfect redemption would come.

All these things were quietly talked about, the news passing from ear to ear, so as not to cause a stir among women and uneducated men, whose understanding was limited. Nevertheless, the common people, too, had their own way of predicting the help that would surely come to the Jews.

In almost every town one person ran about testifying that the Jews would all soon be redeemed. Some declared that they could hear the great ram's horn being blown, signifying the end of days; others aroused the people to return to God, reckoning up their own as well as the sins of others; still others danced in the street for joy, and beat drums.

Ordinary women dreamed remarkable dreams. Dead kin told them all about the wonders that would soon occur. Sleeping and waking, people saw, riding an ass, that pauper who was to be the Messiah; they heard Elijah the Prophet call: "Redemption cometh to the world!" A great cloud lowered, and all the

Jews with their wives and children sat on it to fly to Jerusalem. Before them flew their prayer houses and study houses. A servant girl from Bechev related how, dozing, she had seen a fiery building as high as heaven, and bright as the sun. Around it, Jews in silken garments, wearing the fur caps of the devout, kneeled and sang the Sabbath psalms of praise. Her master, a learned man, immediately understood that the girl had been considered worthy to glimpse the heavenly Temple, with the Levites in attendance; he had made the rounds of the communities with her, that she might describe her vision. Gentile soothsayers divulged that more than once they had observed, in the eastern sky, a tiny star at war with all the others, gradually assimilating them and waxing larger until it became the size of the moon. This was taken as a sign that the smallest and most humble of nations would overcome the peoples of the earth and rule them. Priests, also, testified that they had seen the battle of Armageddon waged in Heaven, with Israel victorious.

Incomprehensible things occurred everywhere. Vagabonds who wandered from town to town and from land to land told of a hail of flintstones that had fallen in Bohemia. During a rainstorm in Turkey a gigantic snake had slithered from the sky, overwhelmed a number of cities, and killed many Jew-haters. In Shebreshin a water carrier had heard a heavenly voice, and in Pulav a fish had cried, "Hear, O Israel!" while being scaled in honor of the Sabbath eve dinner. Some had heard a voice from Mount Horeb crying, "Return, O my wayward children!" A sinful leech, to whom this heavenly voice came three times running, deserted his wife and children, girded sackcloth on his loins, and went into exile. He lay down on the threshold of the study house in every town he came to, and all who entered or left had to step on him and spit in his face, while he, sobbingly, confessed all his misdeeds. A great deal of emphasis was placed on the fact that in these dreadful times, when Jews were being tormented and driven out of town after town, the number of converts from Christianity increased in every land. Very often, converts had themselves circumcized secretly and took on the yoke of the holy teachings, despite the harsh punishment this brought. These were all distinct omens that an end was coming to the long, dark night of servitude, and that the time of liberation was drawing near.

But people most often spoke of one great and holy man, Sabbatai Zevi, who was said to be the one for whom Israel had been waiting these seventeen hundred years and who would be revealed in a short time. Some insisted that he was Messiah, the son of Joseph, who, as the holy volumes indicated, was to be killed as the precursor of the true Messiah; others argued that Messiah, the son of Joseph, had already come in the person of one Reb Abraham Zalman, who had perished in Tishevitz, martyred for the sanctification of God's name, and that Sabbatai Zevi would be the true Messiah, the son of David. Various rumors concerning him were passed around. Some said that he dwelt in a palace in Jerusalem, others that he hid with his disciples in a deep cave; some knew as a fact that he rode daily on a silk-saddled horse with fifty runners before him—others, that he fasted from Sabbath to Sabbath and wracked his body with the most severe torments. Every emissary brought another story. A Frank who had wandered to Lublin swore that Sabbatai Zevi was as tall as a cedar, wore gold, silver, and precious stones, and that it was impossible to look at his face because of its brilliance. A Talmud scholar from some distant place revealed that Sabbatai Zevi was involved in a controversy with the rabbis, and that they had laid a ban on him, for blasphemy. People also had much to say about Sarah, the girl from Poland, who having fled the Cossacks had prophesied that she was destined to be the Messiah's wife—and had married Sabbatai Zevi. While some declared she was modest and God-fearing, others whispered that she had been a whore.

Rabbi Benish knew of these rumors and tales, but he heeded the verse in Amos: "Therefore the prudent doth keep silence in such a time"—and he kept silent. As long as Rabbi Benish dwelt in Lublin he pretended to hear nothing. For many years he had known that Polish Jewry was taking the wrong path. They delved too deeply into things that were meant to be hidden, they drank too little from the clear waters of the holy teachings. The study of the Bible and Hebrew was looked down upon. The early commentators were rarely read. Young men, confused by the twists and turns of *pilpul*, sought to resolve a hundred dilemmas with one answer; they scorned true learning, as child's play. Boys not yet twenty, still young in understanding, were already poring over mystical works, like the Treasury of Life, and Raziel the Angel, and the Zohar, and the interpretations of the mysteries of the Divine Chariot in the Book of Ezekiel. Men deserted their families and wandered through the world, purifying their souls by exile; boys of thirteen immersed themselves in cold baths. There were too many ascetics among Polish Jewry, too many recluses, amulet writers, and wonder workers. Himself a student of philosophy, well versed in The Guide for the Perplexed, and the Cuzari, and the Duties of the Heart, and Principia, Rabbi Benish deplored the cabalistic works of Rabbi Isaac Luria; in his opinion they were contradictory and lewd. Before 1648, when at home in Goray, Rabbi Benish had kept his eyes open and had seen to it that this plague (as he sometimes called it in his thoughts) did not spread. Secretly he had taken the cabalistic volumes with their wooden covers from the study house and had hidden them in his own home. He recited the lessons for the older boys himself, to be sure that they understood the meaning clearly; and he did not allow them to indulge in *pilpul*. Rabbi Benish ordered them to read the biblical Prophets and Writings until they had memorized them, and he taught the boys Hebrew grammar, although in Poland this was considered almost apostasy. If a younger rabbi had dared this, he would have been driven from the town. But Rabbi Benish Ashkenazi was respected. The substantial citizens—men of means who liked common sense and moderation in all things—stood by Rabbi Benish in his battle against the zealots. The young man who secluded himself to become immersed in the study of the mysteries would be flogged, or forbidden to appear in the prayer house, until he stood before the congregation in his stockinged feet and promised no longer to isolate himself from the community. Occasionally, adepts in the cabala, men who could extract wine from walls, heal the sick, and even revive the dead, would appear in Goray. But Rabbi Benish did not permit them to stay long. Those who refused to leave of their own accord would be forced to leave. There would be a certain amount of grumbling, Rabbi Benish's foes claiming that he disbelieved in the cabala.

Once unknown persons posted a paper slandering Rabbi Benish. But the rabbi remained steadfast in his ways, maintaining, "So long as I live, there will be no idolatry in Goray!"

To Rabbi Benish the misfortunes of the years 1648 and 1649 were a punishment visited on Polish Jews because they had been unfaithful to the Law; he was certain that, once the persecutions were over, they would return to the ways of their fathers. But now that their afflictions were past and his expectations were not fulfilled, the rabbi shrank into himself and said nothing. For he perceived that divine providence willed otherwise; as he did not know what Heaven wished, he humbly acquiesced. Each day brought its news, never anticipated, never the same, often contradicting that of the day before. More and more, Jews divided into sects. Even the great rabbis could not agree. Nor was this age of sickness and catastrophe the time to harangue the people.

And Rabbi Benish returned from Lublin, to the town that lay in the midst of the hills, half in ruins and cut off from the world. There the old man immured himself as within an ark, to endure the bad years in solitude. Only on rare occasions did Rabbi Benish cross the threshold of his house. He would glance about him, and inquire of a passing porter or school boy:

"How will it end?"

"What does God want?"

✿ 4 ✿

The Old Goray and the New

October 1666. The rain had been coming down in
torrents for a week, and every night that week the
wind had blown as fiercely as though seven witches
had hanged themselves. The downpour had flooded
cellars, washed plaster off walls, put out fires in ovens.
In the woods many trees were uprooted. The swift
stream that ran near Goray had been blocked in its
course and had overflowed the low places. The windmill sails had been torn from their chains, hence meal
was dear. The few who were well off in Goray and
who had laid in stocks of food during the summer

months remained secluded at home, fearful of worshiping in congregation, lest they see the misery of the poor and hear their complaints. They dozed under goosefeather comforters, relished hot grits, smoked tobacco, dreamed of the fairs of old, and the mad, spendthrift gentry. For fear of thieves, they lit no lamps at night and would, at the slightest provocation, have buried their property and goods in the earth and made off. On the stoves of the poor, the pots stood empty and cold. The roads were dangerous, and no wagons dared venture into town. On rare occasions, a peasant carrying a small bag on his back would swim into view. He would sink above his knees in the mud, and plod from shop to shop, deliberating over where to sell his handful of rye. Women in mannish boots, their heads covered with torn shawls, would crawl forth to meet him like worms emerging from their holes. Tugging at his arms they would bargain for hours, until their toothless mouths became blue with cold.

"A black year on you, dear sir," they would cajole, mockingly, half in Yiddish, half in Ukranian. "Pharaoh's plagues fall on your head!"

Goray was unquiet. A runner who had left for a distant village a day after the Feast of Tabernacles had not returned, and it was said that for his thirty-odd groschen the peasants had murdered him. Only by a miracle had a youth who traveled from farm to farm buying up produce escaped disaster. Spending the night in the silo of a peasant he had been wakened by the sound of his host murderously sharpening a hatchet. The feeble wasted away, and one by one they died. Each death brought Grunam the Beadle running through town in the early morning. Hurriedly, he would rap twice on each shutter with his wooden mallet, as a sign that the water was to be poured out of the house's water-run to thwart evil spirits (that no evil spirits might be mirrored there) and the household was to prepare for a funeral.

Rabbi Benish labored to be with the poor in their hour of need. He issued a decree that the wealthy must share a tithe of their bread and grits, yellow peas and beans, linseed oil, and cords of wood. Tuesdays, two public-spirited citizens made the rounds of the town with a bag for the tithe; but the high cost of things had made people mean, and they hid their food. There should have been no lack of meat, since calves were cheap. But the old slaughterer had been killed, and no new one had settled in Goray. Anyone who wanted to slaughter a beast had to drive it to a slaughterhouse miles away.

The old Jewish town of Goray was unrecognizable. Once upon a time everything had proceeded in an orderly fashion. Masters had labored alongside their apprentices, and merchants had traded; fathers-in-law had provided board and lodging, and sons-in-law had studied the holy teachings; boys had gone off to school, and school mistresses had visited the girls at home. Reb Eleazar Babad and the seven town elders had kept a sharp watch on all town affairs. Those who sinned were brought to court; those who did not obey the court's ruling were flogged, or pilloried in the prayer-house anteroom. On Thursdays and Fridays the needy went from house to house carrying beggars' bags, collecting food for the Sabbath; on the Sabbath itself the good women of the town collected white bread and meat, fish and fruit for the needy. If a poor man had a daughter over fifteen years old who was still unwed, the community contrived to arrange a trousseau, and give her in marriage to an orphan youth or an elderly widower. The money that the groom received at the wedding sufficed to support them for months. After that, the man worked at something or other, or went about the countryside with a writ from the community certifying that he was a pauper. Of course, all sorts of misfortunes occurred. At times man and wife fell to quarreling, and they would have to journey to Yanov for a divorce— for the Goray stream had two names, and no one knew which was the proper one to use in locating Goray in the bill of divorcement according to the strict letter of the law. (*"The town of Goray, on the banks of the River thus-and-thus."*) Sometimes a man would go off, leaving his wife behind him, or be drowned somewhere in some body of endless waters whence his corpse might never be recovered. In such a case the widow could not marry again. Every year before Passover there would be a great furor in Goray over the paschal wheat, which the community would give as a concession to some man of influence—who would eventually always be accused of mixing the meal with chaff before selling it. As a rule, he would be roundly cursed and would not live out the year. Nevertheless, the next year another man was always found to profit from the Passover wheat. Every year on the day of the Rejoicing of the Law, there would be a fight in the tailors' prayer house concerning who was to have the honor of being the first to carry the Torah scroll around the lectern. Afterward the burial society would get drunk at the feast and break dishes. Several times a year there would be an epidemic, and Mendel the Gravedigger would end up with a few extra guilders. But such, after all, is the way of the world. The Jews of Goray dwelled in peace with the village Christians; in the town itself there lived only a few gentiles: a Sabbath gentile, to do the necessary work forbidden Jews on the Sabbath, a bath attendant, and a few others who lived in side streets, their houses surrounded by high picket fences so as not to flaunt their presence.

Before the Christian holidays, when large numbers of gentiles passed through Goray on the way to a shrine, young boys were everywhere industriously selling the pilgrims barrelsful of sweetened water. The Goray fairs were famous throughout the countryside. Peasants from all the nearby villages would come riding for the fair. Horses neighed, cows mooed, goats bleated. Horse traders—powerful Jews dressed in heavy jackets and sheepskin hats summer and winter—leaped to grab kicking stallions. They shouted

as coarsely as any of the peasants. Bloody-handed
butchers, with sharp knives thrust in their belts,
would drag by the horn bound oxen who were no
longer fit for the plow. In those days the grain merchants' bins were always full, and fat, white-bellied
mice dined there; country whiskey at the taverns was
mixed with whole buckets of water. All during the
fair the children of Ham rejoiced in their own way.
They danced with their women, pounding the floor
with their feet, whistling and singing coarse songs.
The women screamed and shook their hips, the men
fought, swinging mighty fists. And what merchandise
did Jews not sell! They sold women's flower-pat-
terned shawls and headkerchiefs; egg rolls and long,
twisted white breads; children's shoes and wading-
boots; spices and nuts; iron yokes and nails; gilded
bridal gifts and ready-made dresses; noisemakers for
night watchmen, and Christmas Eve masks. True,
often enough Rabbi Benish had inderdicted Jews'
dealing in Christian images. Nevertheless, secretly
sales continued of missals with gilded covers and
pages, wax candles and even holy pictures of saints
with halos round their heads. In some out-of-the-
way corner of the fair stood the few Goray gentiles,
selling beet-brown salamis and white hog fat. Once a
fastidious young man passed by them and conspicu-
ously held his nose, as though something smelled;
afterward, he remarked peevishly, "The goy certainly eats well . . . you can smell it for a mile!"

In the evening the sober peasants would ride off.

Drunks would be thrown out of the taverns into the mud, and their angry women would pull them home by the ears. The dark circle of the fair grounds would be covered with dung, and from it would rise the rustic smell of manure. In Jewish homes oil lamps, candles, and pieces of kindling would be lit. Women wearing enormous deep-pocketed aprons would spit on their palms to ward off the evil eye, and feverishly count the copper money they transferred to pots; in houses where there was no counting of money, it was deemed that the blessing of good fortune would be more apt to enter. Goray Jews had great needs. They needed board and lodging for sons-in-law and gifts for bridegrooms; satin dresses and velvet coats for brides and fur hats and silk coats for the men. For the holidays they needed: citrus fruit for the Feast of Tabernacles, the white unleavened bread for Passover, and olive oil for the Feast of Lights. Jews needed money to lend to wicked lords and to silence possible slanderers. More than once it was necessary to send an intercessor to Lublin. And then there were community needs: The town of Goray maintained a rabbi and his assistant, beadles and school teachers, one ritual slaughterer and ten charity scholars, as well as attendants for the bathhouse, one for the men and one for the women, besides the poor and the sick in the infirmary. And how many times did not Goray, this town at the end of the world, have to send money to other communities that had been despoiled or burned down!

In those days Rabbi Benish reigned in Goray like a king. The people went to the rabbi's assistant with their simple questions, and to Rabbi Benish only when they were difficult, or involved suits of law. Rabbi Benish would roll up the sleeves of his coat, and rule according to the strict letter of the law, reckoning with no one. More than one Sabbath eve Grunam the Beadle had to go rapping from shutter to shutter with the news that the bathhouse was unclean, and the men were to stay away from the women who had been there that day. Often Rabbi Benish discovered too late that he had ruled an animal kosher when it was not. Half of the housewives of the town then had to smash their earthen vessels, scald the iron ones, and pour the soup and meat into the swill heap. Living was easy, and Jewishness in high repute those days.

But now Goray had fallen upon evil days. Its best citizens had been slaughtered. Most of the men who remained were young. Though the land was quiet, the fear of new visitations never left the Jews. Worst of all, at this time when unity was most necessary, every man went his own way, no longer willing to share the common responsibility. Time and again Rabbi Benish called a town meeting, only to have the townspeople doze off, or yawn at the walls. They would agree to everything, but carry out nothing. It was almost impossible to find anyone he could speak to. Rabbi Benish thought of his sons, but he had never detested them so much as he did now. Ozer, that scatterbrain, sat for days on end in the kitchen, disheveled and covered with feathers, playing Goats and Wolves with his own children, and quarreling with his mother because she would not cook the dishes he liked. Levi and his wife, like two great spiders spinning an evil web, sat apart from the rest in a pique in their darkened room, where the curtains were always drawn and the door always closed.

❦ 5 ❦

The Woman and the Rabbinical Emissary

The rumor that the days of the Messiah were drawing near gradually aroused even Goray, that town in the midst of the hills at the end of the world.

A highly respectable woman, who for many years now had been journeying in search of her husband (collecting alms at the same time), related that in all the provinces of Poland people were saying that the Exile had come to an end. Trees had begun to put forth enormous fruit in the holy land, and in the salt waters of the Dead Sea golden fish had suddenly appeared. The woman went from house to house. Her face was wrinkled like a cabbage head, but her black eyes were young and gleaming. The satin bands that hung down from her high bonnet rustled, the long earrings in her lobes swayed, and her lips—thin and keen—uttered assurances of salvation and consolation. Everywhere the woman tasted preserves which diligent housewives had put up in the summertime; blew her crooked, rabbinical nose; and with the silken tucks of her sleeve wiped the tears that slid brightly down her withered cheeks to shine among all the ornaments on the voluminous satin coat. The woman smelled of honey cake and holiday, of remote Jewish cities and good tidings. Chatting about the Land of Israel as though she had just returned from there, she told how the holy soil, which had been shrunken like a deer skin, now expanded day by day. The mosques were sinking into the earth, and the Turks were running away or being converted while there was still time, for later, after the Messiah came, no converts would be accepted. Even in Poland the nobles were showing favor to the Jews and showering them with gifts, having already heard that the children of Israel were soon to be exalted above all peoples. Crowds of women followed her about, tirelessly asking question after question—and she replied in phrases from the holy tongue, like a man. Wealthy folk presented her with gold pieces, which she painstakingly and piously bound into a kerchief, as though she were collecting donations for strangers.

When Rabbi Benish heard about the woman he sent for her to present herself, but it was too late, for she was already in her sleigh, prepared to ride off. The people of Goray had wrapped blankets around her and covered her with straw; they gave her jugs of cherry juice and Sabbath cookies. Her ram's-horn nose was red with the cold and the fear of God, and she replied to the beadle: "Tell the rabbi that, God-willing, we shall yet meet in the Land of Israel . . . at the gates of the Holy Temple."

A traveling man who used to visit Goray yearly even before 1648 passed along the news that in Volhynia Jews were dancing for joy in the streets. They had stopped buying houses and sewing heavy overcoats, since it would be warm in the Land of Israel. In-laws-to-be were postponing weddings, so as to be able to raise the bridal canopy in Jerusalem. In Narol the young men had begun to study the Jerusalem Talmud, in preference to the Babylonian, and a rich man in Masel-Bozhitz had divided his possessions among the poor.

An ascetic who ate no meat, drank no wine, slept on a hard bench, and journeyed over the world on foot, related that a prophet named Reb Nehemiah ha-Cohen had arisen in Poland Minor. He wore a haircloak over his bare skin, and, prophesying, would fall face down to the earth, emitting cries that were more than human. Reb Nehemiah foretold that the Jews were soon to foregather from all the corners of the earth, and the dead would rise from their graves.

The greatest rabbis and men of genius believed in this prophet and gave him tokens of their esteem.

But he who raised the tumult in Goray to its highest pitch was a certain rabbinical legate, a Jew from Yemen.

It was midwinter, early one January evening. All day a wind had been blowing, driving hills of snow and piling them up in front of the houses—blue, glassy, filling the air with dust, as in a field. Crows waddled about on their short feet, picked at a frozen cat, cawed with their crooked beaks, and flew low in the air to exercise their wings. Few windowpanes remained whole in their frames, and on these grew complicated frost patterns of trees that seemed to have been turned upside down by the storm, their stocks broken. The roofs hung low, stooping to the earth, and a column of milk-white smoke spiraled from every chimney, as though boring into the sky. God's stars trembled brighter and larger than usual, sparkling green and blue in the atmosphere. Circled by three pearl halos that reflected all the colors of the rainbow, a yellow moon, like an eye, looked down at the Jews hurrying to their afternoon prayers. Suddenly the sharp clanging of a bell was heard in the market place, and a sleigh drove up. A man with a snow-covered beard and long earlocks got out. He was wearing a red turban and a fur coat turned inside out. Darting fiery glances everywhere with his black eyes, he asked: "Where is the study house?"

The newcomer appeared in the holy place between

the afternoon and evening prayers. His arrival created a sensation. He stopped at the threshold, where he pulled off his felt shoes and stood in stockinged feet. Afterward, he removed his outer garment, revealing a long smock black-striped like a prayer shawl, and girdled about with an embroidered sash. Washing his hands and feet for a long time at the copper water tap, the newcomer recited a benediction in a language that sounded like Aramaic. Then, ascending the dais with measured step, he turned his face to the eastern wall, and cried out in a trembling voice: "Judeans, I come to bring you good tidings! From Jerusalem our holy city!"

The newcomer's arrival immediately became known in town, and a throng came running to the study house. Womenfolk mingled with menfolk, young men and girls stood up together on reading stands and tables. Everyone gaped and listened. The stranger spoke in a broken voice, one that seemed to be full of tears:

"Judeans," he said, "I come from our holy land. I am a pure-blooded Sephardi. I have been sent by my brothers into the Exile, to tell you that the Great Fish that lurks in the river Nile has succumbed at the hands of Sabbatai Zevi, our Messiah and holy king. . . . His kingship will soon be revealed, and he will take the sultan's crown from off his head. . . . The Jews from the other side of the river Sambation are ready and waiting for the battle of Armageddon. . . . The lion that dwelleth on high will descend

from Heaven, in his mouth a seven-headed scorpion.
. . . With fire issuing from his nostrils, he will carry
the Messiah into Jerusalem. Gather your strength,
O Judeans, and make yourselves ready! . . . Happy
is the man who shall live to see this!"

The study house became so quiet that a solitary fly
could be heard buzzing, beating its wings against the
window. Women wrung their hands, and from their
grimaces it was difficult to tell whether they were
laughing or weeping. There was a sea of startled
faces. The crowd stirred, as when the ram's horn is
blown on Rosh Hashana. The legate looked about
him.

"Wonders and miracles are performed in Jerusalem. . . . In Miron a fiery column has been seen
stretching from earth to heaven. . . . The full name
of God and of Sabbatai Zevi were scratched on it in
black. . . . The women who divine by consulting
drops of oil have seen the crown of King David on
Sabbatai Zevi's head. . . . Many disbelievers deny
this and refuse to turn back at the very threshold of
Gehenna. . . . Woe unto them! They will sink and
be lost in the nethermost circle of Sheol!"

"Jews! Save your-selves! Jew-ws!" someone suddenly shouted, as though he were choking.

The crowd shuddered. It was lame Mordecai
Joseph, a cabalist, with a thick, fiery beard and bushy
eyebrows, a faster, a weeper, an angry man. As he
prayed he would beat his head against the wall; on
the Days of Awe he would fall to the ground at the
Prayer of Petition, like the men of old, and groan

out loud. He delivered funeral orations and on the eve of Yom Kippur flogged men in the prayer-house anteroom. When he fell into a fierce mood he would slap not only the young but the old as well; therefore none dared cross him. Mordecai Joseph was broad-framed, ungainly, with unkempt red earlocks and green eyes. And now, breathing hard, the cripple began to clamber up a table. Those close by lifted him so that he could stand. Reb Mordecai Joseph banged the table with his crutch. His stained coat came unbuttoned, his unkempt locks flew about wildly, and he began in his passion to stutter and gasp.

"Jews, why are you silent? Redemption hath come to the world! . . . Salvation hath come to the world!"

He beat his forehead with his left hand and all at once began to dance. His oaken crutch drummed, his large foot dangled, and, gasping, he cried one and the same phrase over and over again, a phrase which no one was able to make out.

The legate turned and fixed his bright eyes on Mordecai Joseph. The tails of Mordecai Joseph's coat swung through the air, his vest billowed about him; he pushed the crumpled skullcap back on his head, stretched out both arms, the fingers curling. Women screamed; from every side hands reached for him. Suddenly Reb Mordecai fell his full length to the ground. The whole study house swayed with the crowd and the sweating walls. Someone shouted, "Help! He has fainted!"

❦ 6 ❦

Reb Mordecai Joseph

It was Rabbi Benish's practice to say his afternoon
and evening prayers by himself in his study. When
the news reached his ears he hurried to the prayer
house. But it was already empty. Everyone had
hurried home after the legate's sermon to discuss
the news in the midst of the family. A few people
accompanied the legate to the inn; others went to
the house of Reb Mordecai Joseph. They had to rub
Mordecai Joseph with snow for a long time, to prick
him with needles and pinch him hard before he was

himself again. On his broken bench bed he lay, dressed in all his garments; leaning back on both elbows, he related that in his trance Sabbatai Zevi had come to him and cried: "Mordecai Joseph, the son of Chanina the Priest, be not of humble heart! Thou shalt yet offer up the priestly sacrifices!" Men and women jostled one another in the narrow, unfloored room; there was no candle, and Mordecai Joseph's wife heaped several dry twigs on the tripod and lit them. The flame crackled and hissed, red shadows danced on the irregular whitewashed walls, and the rafters loomed low. In a corner, on a pile of rags, sat Mordecai Joseph's only daughter, a monstrosity with a water-swollen head and calf's eyes. Mordecai Joseph's wet beard shone in the reflection of the glowing coals like molten gold, and his green eyeballs burned like a wolf's as he divulged the mysteries he had seen in his trance. His cadence was that of a dying man speaking his last words to those nearest him.

"A great light shall descend on the world! Thousands and thousands times greater than the sun! It shall blind the eyes of the wicked and the scoffers! Only the chosen shall escape!"

That night Rabbi Benish could not sleep.

The shutters were barred, and thick candles burned in the two bent brass candlesticks. The old man paced back and forth with heavy tread, stopping from time to time to cock his ears, as though listening for a scratching in the walls. The wind tore at

the roof, and sighed. Branches crackled with the
frost, the long-drawn-out howls of dogs filled the air.
There was silence and then the howling began again.
Rabbi Benish took book after book out of the chest,
studied their titles and leafed through the pages
searching for omens of the coming of the Messiah.
His high forehead wrinkled, for the passages were
contradictory. From time to time Rabbi Benish
would sit down at the table and press a key to his
forehead so as not to doze off; nevertheless, he would
soon be snoring heavily. Then he would lift his head
up with a start, a crooked mark between his eyes. He
paced back and forth, running into objects in dark
corners, and his magnified shadow crept along the
rafters, slid along the walls, and quivered as though
engaged in a ghostly wrangle. Although the oven was
glowing, a cold breeze stirred in the room. In the
early morning, when Grunam the Beadle came to
put more wood in the oven, Rabbi Benish looked at
him as though he were a stranger.

"Go, bring the legate to me!" he commanded.

The legate was still sleeping in the inn, and
Grunam had to waken him. It was early, and stars
were still sparkling in the sky. Handfuls of dry salt-
like snow fell across their faces. Rabbi Benish put
on his outercoat and stepped over the threshold of
the house to welcome the legate; putting up his
beaver collar and crossing his arms, he thrust his
hands up his sleeves. It was bitter cold and Rabbi
Benish kept turning around, stamping his feet to

keep warm. Somewhere from behind the snow hills, as huge as sand dunes, a man rose into view, wind-blown, dipped out of sight, and then emerged again, like a swimmer. Rabbi Benish glanced at the early morning sky. Fixing his gaze inwardly, he cried, "Master of the Universe, help us!"

No one ever learned what Rabbi Benish said that morning, nor what the legate replied. But one thing soon became common knowledge: the legate rode away with no farewells from Goray, in the same sleigh in which he had arrived. It was late after-noon when the news spread that the legate had disappeared. It was Grunam the Beadle who im-parted the information, with a stealthy smile in his left eye. Reb Mordecai Joseph blanched. He gathered immediately who was responsible for the legate's de-parture, and his nostrils dilated with anger.

"Benish is to blame!" he screamed, and lifted his crutch threateningly. "Benish has driven him off!"

For many years Reb Mordecai Joseph had been the rabbi's enemy. He hated him for his learning, envied him his fame, and never missed an oppor-tunity to speak evil of him. At the yearly Passover wrangle he would incite the people to break Rabbi Benish's windowpanes, crying that the rabbi had only his own reputation in mind and gave no thought to the town. The thing that chiefly vexed Reb Mordecai Joseph was that Rabbi Benish forbade the study of the cabala; in defiance Reb Mordecai Joseph called the rabbi by his first name. And now Reb Mordecai

Joseph hammered on his lectern, inciting controversy.

"Benish is a heretic!" he shouted. "A transgressor against the Lord of Israel!"

An old householder who was one of the rabbi's disciples ran over to Mordecai Joseph and struck him twice. The blood streamed from Mordecai Joseph's nose. Several young people jumped up and grabbed their belts. The cantor pounded on the stand, and commanded them not to interrupt the prayers, but he was ignored. Men wearing the large black phylacteries on their heads, and with the broad phylactery thongs wound around their arms, milled about, pushing one another. A tall, black-complexioned man, whose head almost reached the ceiling, began to waver like a tree in the wind, and cried: "Sacrilege! Blood in the study house! Woe!"

"Benish is a heretic!" roared Mordecai Joseph.

Holding on to his crutch he bent over and hopped forward with insane speed.

"May he be torn from the earth . . . root and all!"

Drops of blood shimmered on his fire-red beard; his low forehead, parchment-yellow, was furrowed. Reb Senderel of Zhilkov, an ancient foe of the rabbi, suddenly screamed: "Rabbi Benish cannot oppose the world! He has always been a man of little faith!"

"Apostate!" someone shouted, it was hard to tell whether referring to the rabbi or his opponents.

"Disrupter!"

"Sinner that leadeth the multitude to sin!"

"The world's aflame!" Mordecai Joseph kept

pounding with his fists. "Benish, the dog, denies the Messiah!"

"Sabbatai Zevi is a false Messiah!" a high, boyish voice cried out.

Everyone looked around. It was Chanina, the charity scholar, a young divorced man and a stranger, who sat in Goray studying and lived off the community. He was one of Rabbi Benish's brilliant students—tall, overgrown, nearsighted, with a long, pale face and a chin sprouting with yellow hair. His coat was always unfastened, his vest open, showing a thin, hairy chest. Now he stood there, bent over his study stand, his near-blind eyes blinking, waiting with a silly smile for someone to come and argue with him, so that he could show how learned he was. Mordecai Joseph, who bore Chanina a grudge on account of the many folios of the Talmud he knew by heart and because he was always mixing in where he had no right, suddenly sprang at Chanina with that agility the lame display when they flare up and forget their defect.

"You, too!" he screamed. "Take him, men!"

Several young men ran over to Chanina, grabbed hold of his shirt and began to drag him off. Chanina opened his mouth, shouted, tried to tear himself loose from their grip, twisted his long neck back and forth, and flailed about him with his arms, like a drowning man. His coat was torn, his skull cap fell off. Two long, tousled earlocks dangled from his shaven scalp. He tried to defend himself, but the charity students were quick to hold his head, punching him with their weak hands as they helped carry him, as though they were kneading dough. Mordecai Joseph himself proudly helped carry Chanina by the legs, spitting into his face and pinching him viciously. Soon Chanina was lying on the table. They lifted his coat tail. Mordecai Joseph was the first to do the honors.

"Let this be in place of me!" he cried, in the words of the Yom Kippur scapegoat ritual. He rolled up his sleeves, and gave Chanina so hard a blow that the unlucky youth burst all at once into tears, like a school boy, and whimpered.

"Let this be instead of me!" Mordecai Joseph exclaimed with a sigh and again struck Chanina.

"Let this fowl go to his death!" someone cried responsively, and a hail of blows fell on the idle scholar. Chanina gave a hoarse cry and began to gasp.

When they took him from the table, his face was blue and his mouth clenched. A boy immediately fetched a vessel of water and poured it over Chanina, drenching him from head to foot. The young man jerked spasmodically and remained full length on the ground. There was a terrified silence in the study house. The one woman who happened to be in the women's gallery pulled at the grate and sobbed. Mordecai Joseph limped back, beating the floor with his crutch, and his face behind the thicket of his beard was chalk-white.

"Thus rotteth the name of the wicked!" he said. "Now he shall know that there is a God who rules the world!"

❦ 7 ❦

Reb Eleazar Babad and His Daughter, Rechele

Reb Eleazar Babad was seldom at home. It was his practice to move about from village to village. He would put on his heavy coat, stuff straw in his shoes, and, with a sack in one hand, a stick in the other, take to the paths and byways. Like a beggar he would drive off the hounds with his stick and sleep nights in the haylofts of peasant barns. Some said that Reb Eleazar went to collect old debts due him from before 1648; others were certain that he wandered this way as a penance for the sins that were wearying his spirit. Rechele, his only daughter, remained at home

all alone. For days on end she sat on a foot bench
facing the hearth, reading the volumes she had
brought from distant cities, and it was rumored that
she was versed in the holy tongue. Some even went so
far as to declare that she had learned Latin from a
physician in Lublin. Goray housewives had sought to
be friendly with Rechele and had paid her courtesy vis-
its, but her response had not been the usual "God bid
ye welcome." She had not urged them to be seated but
had hid something from them in the bosom of her
dress. Young matrons in silk bonnets, usually with
aprons bulging over their pregnant bellies, came to
amuse Rechele, to play at bones with her, and to chat
about prospective matches, as young women will.
Some of them brought their jewels along in caskets
in order to preen themselves; others had balls of wool
and knitting needles, to show how capable they were.
But Rechele sat at the hearth, never rising to greet
them, not even wiping the benches dry for them to
sit upon. She confused their names, acted so haughtily that the women began to laugh and mock her.
Before leaving, the last of the visitors called to
Rechele from the other side of the door: "Don't be
so high and mighty, Rechele! Your father isn't rich
any longer; you're a pauper now!"

Rechele (God save us!) was sickly, and much had
to be forgiven her. The woman who went from house
to house Thursdays to knead the troughs of dough
for the Sabbath reported that Rechele ate less than a
fly; she had her period every three months. She slept

late in the morning and barricaded her door at night with wooden crossbars. A neighbor that lived behind Reb Eleazar's brick house in a dwelling that had half settled in the earth whispered that Rechele never went into the yard to relieve herself. . . .

Rechele had been born in Goray in 1648, a few weeks before the massacre. When the *haidamaks* had besieged Zamość, her mother had fled with the infant in her arms, and, after many trials, had arrived in Lublin. The little one had been five at her mother's death, and Reb Eleazar had been in Vlodave with the rest of the household at the time. Rechele alone had remained in Lublin at the home of an uncle, Reb Zeydel Ber, who was a ritual slaughterer. He was a tall man with thick eyebrows above red eyes, and a black beard that reached to his waist, a taciturn widower who kept to himself. In the booth in the courtyard where he did his slaughtering there was always a wooden bucket full of blood, and feathers flew about constantly. Here day was as dark as night when a small oil lamp burned. Butcher boys in red-spattered jackets, with knives thrust in their belts, moved about, shouting coarsely. Slaughtered chickens threw themselves to the blood-soaked earth, furiously flapping their pent wings, as though trying to fly off. Calves, whose legs were bound with straw, laid their heads on one another's necks and pounded the earth with their split hooves, until finally their eyes glazed. Once Rechele saw two blood-smeared butcher boys skin a goat and let it lie there with eyeballs protruding in amazement and white teeth projecting in a kind of death-smile.

Rechele was terrified of Reb Zeydel Ber. He had never remarried, and had no children. The house was kept by his mother-in-law, a woman nearly ninety, deaf, with a waxen, shriveled face, full of moles and clumps of yellowish hair. The ancient stone house where they lived had thick walls and small high windows near the vaulted ceiling. It stood somewhere on the edge of town, near the graveyard. The doorway was low and dark as a cave, and faced a dead-end street. The court was rolling and hillocky, full of pits, and all manner of rags, feather dusters, and rotted sacks were scattered about. Reb Zeydel occupied two rooms, with an entrance off a narrow vestibule. He slept in one of the rooms, which had a wide canopy bed hung with faded red satin draperies, a prayer stand, and a book chest. When Uncle was not busy in his slaughter hut he would sit in his bedroom on a shoemaker's round stool and sharpen the greenish blades of his knives on a large, smooth stone. He would test the edges with the nail of his right index finger—allowed to grow long for just that purpose—and listen with his long, hairy ear for sound of a defect in the blade. At other times he would mumble over a holy volume, or prop his forehead on a fist and doze off.

The anteroom held the household necessaries: a water tun and a large vessel for washing pots and dishes, two benches—one for dairy food, the other for

meat—and a broom leaning on a swill heap. The old
woman cooked in a deep sooty oven, constantly occupied with long paddles, and eternally muttering.
Whenever Rechele wanted to go outside to play,
Granny would grab the child with her bony hands,
pull her hair, and hiss at her.

"Sit down, you monster!" she would cry, and pinch
Rechele black and blue. "Throw fits and jump as
high as a house! May the fit carry you off!"

Rechele was a stubborn and contrary child; she
would not let Granny delouse her, and the old woman
had to beat her with a block of wood. In the trough
that held the wash water there was always a switch
soaking with which the old woman would flog the girl
for her wantonness. Every Friday afternoon the old
woman would force Rechele to put her head into
the trough, now filled with hot water, and Rechele
would scream until she was hoarse. To persuade
Rechele to remain at home and not go wandering off,
the old woman took to terrifying the child.

She persuaded Rechele that there were graves in
the yard where ghosts flew about ceaselessly, seeking
bodies to enter. She put a great apron on Rechele as
a charm, so that no unholy spirit might possess her,
and hung a linen sack with a wolf's tooth in it around
her neck. Whenever Granny went away she latched
the door from the outside with a wooden peg. Little
light entered through the small, dust-covered window
near the rafters, and an oil-dipped wick burned constantly in a clay shard. Mice were forever scratching

in the narrow, crowded bedroom, and there were other small sounds as though a hand groped its way through the darkness. There was an opening high above the anteroom hearth. Whenever it smoked a chimney sweep would be summoned, who would scramble up and shout down at the old woman as he worked. His eyes all white as though the eyeballs were turned up, he would grimace blackly, like a devil. Granny would stand below him and shake her small fist.

"Higher!" she would screech. "Higher! Higher!"

Rechele would hide under the bed when the chimney sweep came, burying herself under a pile of clothing. She feared the broom he pulled out of an iron bucket, was terrified of the heavy smoke-covered ropes he uncoiled, would pale when she heard the stranger stumble over the oven. Often there would be two chimney sweeps: the taller had a bristling mustache, like an insect's. One of the sweeps would crawl out on the roof and the other would thrust his head into the hearth opening and cry up to his partner in a muffled voice as though from a cavern. After they had left, the black prints of their bare feet remained on the floor. The slaughterer would come into the room, a knife in a corner of his mouth. His blood-stiff coat covered with feathers would creak as he bent to go through the low door. He would grumble: "How much did you give the dogs?"

"A half penny and a handful of chaff," the old

woman would respond, thrusting out her chin. There was not a tooth in her shrunken mouth.

It was terrifying at night when Rechele had to lie down in the bench-bed to sleep with the old woman. Uncle snored loudly in the bedroom, wheezing as though he choked and groaning in his sleep, and the old woman dallied over her prayers, as she turned restlessly from side to side. She smelled of burned feathers and mice. Sometimes she would lift the child's shift and run her dead hands over the girl's hot body, cackling with impure delight: "Fire! Fire! The girl's burning up!"

As they lay under the feather bed, in the pitch dark, the old woman would tell Rechele stories of wild beasts and goblins; of robbers that lived in caves with witches; of man-eaters that roasted children on spits; and of a wild one-eyed monster that stalked about with a fir tree in its hand looking for a lost princess. Sometimes from her sleep Granny would cry out wildly and incoherently. The roots of Rechele's hair would tingle with terror, and, her whole body a-quiver, she would wake up the old woman with the cry: "Granny? What are you saying? Granny?

"Granny, I'm afraid!"

❦ 8 ❦

Rechele in Lublin

When Rechele was twelve years old the old woman died. For three days she lay on a bench bed in the anteroom, gasping her last. Her small head was bound with a red kerchief, her wrinkled face was stiff as a corpse, her chin pointed up, and her open eyes, with the eyeballs turned back, appeared entirely white. That happened during the Ten Days of Penitence between Rosh Hashana and Yom Kippur. From the slaughter hut in the yard the cackling of roosters could be heard, mingled with the shouting of housewives and servant maids. Rarely did anyone glance in at the dying woman, for everyone was busy. Reb Zeydel Ber, her son-in-law, all smeared with blood, would dash into the anteroom from time to time, beard flying, red eyelids gleaming under bushy eyebrows. Drawing a goosefeather from his breast, he would hold it near the dying woman's nostrils to see whether she was still breathing, examine her expertly, and sigh: "Ah, well, it's a story without an end!"

Uncle Reb Zeydel Ber was as usual before the high holy day, when he was slaughtering atonement roosters whilst the women burdened him with their haste and idle talk. Moreover, young Rechele was burning the meals she cooked for him, because she was tired. Apprehensively she kept the wick burning all night and sat until dawn on the bench enveloped in a shawl. The cricket behind the wall oven chirped even more demandingly than ever. Time and again, from the alcove Uncle would cry out in his sleep, as though he were conversing intermittently with someone. Rechele was well aware that the room was crowded with evil things. The brooms and mops stirred; long shadows swept along the walls like apparitions from another world. Now and again the old woman raised her upper lip in a horrifying smile. She thrust out her waxen hand from under the feather bed, clutched at the air, and then clenched her fingers as though she had caught something. The old woman died in the early morning on the day before Yom Kippur. At once diligent women from the burial society arrived, wearing enormous aprons that encircled their bodies. They heated kettles of water for the ritual of purification, and the room was filled with thick steam, wet rags, and straw. One woman opened the chest and drew out a suit of full under-hose that had been sewed in a shroud stitch and a mitre, which the old woman had prepared in advance; another woman carried a black stretcher into the room. Rechele was sent off to a distant relation of Reb Zeydel Ber's. The funeral took place at once and Reb Zeydel Ber recited the mourner's prayer. Just before sundown Uncle sent for Rechele to be brought home. The wet floor had already been swept and spread with sand. Three candles in memory of Granny's soul were burning in a sand-filled box. Uncle stood in a white smock, wearing cloth shoes, his head covered by a white mitre that was embroidered with golden fringe. His black beard was combed and wet, his earlocks, as long as braids, were still dripping from the bath. He resembled one of those holy and God-fearing Masters of whom Rechele had read in her little books in Yiddish. He placed both hands on her head and said in a sorrowful voice, "May the Lord make thee as Sarah, Rebecca, Rachel, Leah. . . . Be Blessed and of pure spirit, O child, and tend to the house . . . in God's Name!" Rechele opened her lips to answer, but Uncle violently thrust the door open, and rushed out, almost extinguishing the candles. Rechele remained standing in the middle of the room; she looked about in amazement, as though in a strange place. A blood-red fragment of the sky filled the small window near the rafters, and outside a great wailing was heard. Lublin's narrow streets, lighted by the setting sun, were now full of men wearing the white Yom Kippur robes; they looked like corpses in shrouds. The women wore white dresses with trains, and silk scarves; they were arrayed in pearls and heavy necklaces, pins and bracelets, brooches and long earrings which quivered like jelly. Those women who had been widowed or had lost children recently ran with outstretched arms, as though insane, hoarsely repeating the same phrase over and over. Neighbors who had been at each other's throats throughout the year embraced and clung swaying to and fro, as though nothing could separate them. . . . Young matrons walked proudly, holding in one hand the gold-trimmed prayer books while the other caught up the trains of their gowns. Laughing and crying they fell upon each other's necks. Four girls conveyed a paralyzed dowager some hundred years old on a red-upholstered chair. The old woman's golden dress blazed in the sunset and her high bonnet set with beads and precious stones glittered, its satin ribbons fluttering in the wind. A blind old man, with a white wind-blown beard, stood leaning on his crutches, his blue hands groping to bless all who passed by. The street leading to the prayer house was filled with low tables on which stood alms bowls. The crooked, the dumb, the lame sat on footstools and counted the silver and copper coins with which the crowd redeemed their souls for the holy day. Yerucham, the Lublin Penitent, stood as he did every year, at the door of the prayer house barefoot, his clothes unfastened. Wringing his hands, he wept for his sins.

"Jews, have mercy, Jew-ws! . . . Com-passion. . . . Com-passion! . . ."

But here, in this lonely street, inside the thick walls, Rechele heard only an echo. She stood there, ears cocked and eyes wide. This was her first time alone on Yom Kippur eve. In the past Granny had invited girls in to sit with her, and they would pass the evening braiding each other's hair and talking in hushed voices while huddled at the table. The night before Yom Kippur is a frightening time. Often, on that night, lords would fall upon Jewish homes and ravish the young, unprotected girls. Sometimes the candles would droop, and the children alone in the house would have to run outside to find a gentile to straighten them. Fires in which small children perished were frequent. Everyone remembered the catastrophe in the great synagogue when someone had called out that the city was on fire and in the panic many men and women had been trampled on and crushed. Moreover, it was common knowledge that on this, the holiest of nights, when the awesome prayer of Kol Nidre was chanted, the air was full of those ghosts that could find no resting place in the Hereafter. Rechele and her friends had once seen with their own eyes such a ghost pass by the candle and disappear in the hearth. . . . The candle flame smoked and sputtered for a long time afterward.

Now Rechele was alone in the house on the night before Yom Kippur, and only a few hours previously a corpse had been taken away.

Rechele wanted to go out into the street and call people to her, but she was afraid to open the door in the dark passageway. She pursed her lips to shout, but the cry would not leave her throat. Terrified, she threw herself on the bench-bed, rolled up into a ball, shut her eyes, and covered herself with the comforter. From somewhere a low mutter reached her ears. The sound seemed to come from beneath the earth, and it appeared to Rechele that it was the chanting of Kol Nidre. But then it dawned on her that it was the dead who were chanting, and she knew that whosoever hears the Kol Nidre of the dead would not live out the year.

She fell asleep and in her dreams Granny came to her—her clothes in tatters, disheveled and haggard. The kerchief about her head was soaked with blood. "Rechele! Rechele!" she screamed and rubbed the girl's face with a straw whisk.

Rechele's whole body shuddered. She awoke, drenched with sweat. There was a ringing in her ear, and she felt a sharp stab in her breast. She tried to cry but could not. Gradually, the terror subsided. She heard footsteps in the house, fragmentary phrases. The pots on the oven and on the benches moved and were suspended in air. The candle box turned around and did a jig. There was a scarlet glow on the walls. Everything seethed, burst, crackled, as though the whole house were aflame. . . . Late that night, when Uncle came home, he found Rechele lying with her knees pulled to her chest, her eyes glazed and her teeth clenched. Reb Zeydel Ber screamed and people came running. They forced open the girl's mouth and poured sour wine down her throat. A woman skilled in such things scratched Rechele's face with her nails and tore from her head patches of hair. At length Rechele began to groan, but from that evening on she was never the same.

In the beginning Rechele could not speak at all. Later she regained her speech, but she suffered from all sorts of illnesses. Reb Zeydel Ber wished to marry Rechele because she was beautiful and of good family, and he looked after her as though she were his own daughter. He hired a servant maid to care for her, and he had recourse to various cures and charms. A woman was brought in to drive the evil spirit away by incantation; another washed her body with urine; still another applied leeches. Rechele lay inert on her bed. So that she might forget her pain, Reb Zeydel Ber brought her books and even went so far as to instruct her in the Torah. Sometimes the Polish physician who bled Rechele read with her from a Latin book. Eventually Rechele improved and could once more stand, but her left leg continued paralyzed, and she walked with a limp. Then Reb Zeydel Ber died, and Rechele returned to her father, Reb Eleazar

Babad, who in the meantime had lost both wife and son.

Thenceforth Rechele was one apart. She was beset by mysterious ills. Some said she suffered from the falling sickness, others that she was in the power of demons. In Goray Reb Eleazar left her completely on her own, rarely returning from his round of the villages to see her. When people spoke to him about his poor orphan daughter, he would hang his head and answer in confusion:

"Well, let it be . . . ! There is no wisdom nor understanding nor counsel against the Lord!"

❦ 9 ❦

Reb Itche Mates, the Packman

A packman came to Goray with a full sack of holy
scripts and fringed vests, phylacteries and skull caps
for pregnant women and oval bone amulets for children, mezuzahs and prayer sashes. Packmen are no-
toriously short-tempered and suffer no one to touch
their merchandise who is disinclined to purchase.
Gingerly, one at a time, the young men approached
the packman, stared curiously at the store of goods
which he spread out on the table, ran their fingers
along the books, and turned the leaves with silent
caution, so as not to arouse his wrath. But apparently

this was a courteous packman. Putting his hands up his sleeves, he allowed the boys to riffle through the books as much as they pleased. A packman comes from the great world, and usually brings with him all sorts of news. People sidled over to him and asked: "What do they call you, stranger?"

"Itche Mates."

"Well, Reb Itche Mates, what's happening in the world?"

"Praised be God."

"Is there talk of help for the Jews?"

"Certainly, everywhere, blessed be God."

"Perhaps you have letters with you and tracts, Reb Itche Mates?"

Reb Itche Mates said nothing, as though he hadn't heard, and they understood at once that these were matters one did not discuss openly. So, murmuring under their breath, they said, "Are you staying here awhile, Reb Itche Mates?"

He was a short man, with a round, straw-colored beard, and appeared to be about forty years old. His dilapidated hat, from which large patches of fur were missing, was pulled down over his damp, rheumy eyes; his thin nose was red with catarrh. He was wearing a long patched coat which reached to the ground. A red kerchief was wound about his loins. The young men rummaged through his books, ripping the uncut pages, and doing all sorts of damage, but the packman made no objection. Mischievous boys played with the embroidered fringed vests and tried on the gilded skull caps. They even dug down deep in the packman's sack and discovered a Book of Esther scroll cased in a wooden tube, a ram's horn, and a small bag containing white, chalky soil from the Land of Israel. Very few people bought, everyone handled the merchandise and seemed to be conspiring to enrage the packman. But he stood woodenly in front of his goods. When they recited the Holy, Holy, Holy, his straw mustaches quivered almost imperceptibly. When asked anything's price he capped his hand to his ear as though he were hard of hearing, thought for a long time, avoiding his questioner's face.

"What does it matter?" he would finally say in a low hoarse voice. "Give as much as you can." And he extended a tin coin box, as though he wasn't really a packman but was collecting money for some holy purpose.

Levi, the rabbi's son, invited him for supper, for in his controversy with his father Levi lent his silent support to the Sabbatai Zevi sect. Gathered together were members of the inner circle; all the cabalists apparently sensed that the packman had something of interest to tell. Reb Mordecai Joseph, Rabbi Benish's foe, was amongst them. Nechele, Levi's wife, closed the shutters and stuffed the keyhole so that Ozer's children would not be able to carry on their customary spying. Everyone sat around the table. Nechele offered them onion flatcakes, and set drinks on the table. Reb Itche Mates took only a morsel of bread, which he swallowed whole, but he bade those about him to feast their fill and drink hearty. Perceiving at once that Reb Itche Mates was one of the chosen, they did as he bade. Their foreheads became moist, and their eyes shone with the hope of great times to come. Reb Itche Mates unbuttoned his jacket and drew from the inner pocket a letter written on parchment in Aramaic, in a scribe's script, and with crownlets on the letters like a Torah scroll. The letter was from Abraham Havchini and Samuel Primo, who resided in the Land of Israel. Hundreds of rabbis had put their signatures to this letter, most of them Sephardim with exotic names reminiscent of the Talmudic masters. It became so quiet that Ozer's boys, who were lurking outside the door, heard not even a whisper. The wick in the shard crackled and sputtered, long shadows trembled on the walls, shook back and forth, merged. The well-born Nechele stood beside the oven where she burnt kindling. Her thin cheeks were flaming hot; she glanced sidelong at the men, and absorbed every word.

Reb Itche Mates sat hunched up, speaking almost in a whisper, divulging mysteries of mysteries: only a few holy sparks still burned among the husks of being. The powers of darkness clung to these, knowing that their existence depended on them. Sabbatai Zevi, God's ally, was battling these powers; it was he who was conducting the sacred sparks back to their primal source. The holy kingdom would be revealed when the last spark was returned whence it had come.

Then the ritual ceremonies would no longer hold. Bodies would become pure spirit. From the World of Emanations and from under the Throne of Glory new souls would descend. There would be no more eating and drinking. Instead of being fruitful and multiplying, beings would unite in combinations of holy letters. The Talmud wouldn't be studied. Of the Bible only the secret essence would remain. Each day would last a year, and the radiance of the holy spirit would fill all space. Cherubim and Ophanim would chant the praise of the Almighty and He Himself would instruct the righteous. Their delight would be boundless.

Reb Itche Mates' speech abounded in homilies and parables from the Torah and Midrash. He was familiar with the names of angels and seraphim, and quoted at length passages from the Book of Transmigrations and Raziel; all the mansions in heaven were known to him, every detail of the supreme hierarchy. There could be no doubt that here was a most holy man, truly one of the elect. The decision was that all should keep silent and that Itche Mates should spend the night at the home of Reb Godel Chasid, who sat opposite. In the morning they would see what was to be done. Reb Godel Chasid took the packman by the hand and led him to his house. He offered him his own bed, but Reb Itche Mates preferred to sleep on the bench near the oven. Reb Godel Chasid gave his guest a sheepskin cover and a pillow and retired to the alcove that served as his bedroom. But he could not sleep. All night long there came from behind the stove a bee-like drone. Reb Itche Mates was busy at Torah and, although there was no window in the room, he was surrounded by light as though the moon shone upon him. Before daybreak Reb Itche Mates rose, poured water on his hands, and sought to steal away to the study house. But Reb Godel Chasid had not undressed. He took Reb Itche Mates by the arm and whispered confidentially, "I saw everything, Reb Itche Mates."

"Ah but what was there to see?" murmured Reb Itche Mates, bowing his head. " 'Silence is seemly for the wise.' "

In the study house Reb Itche Mates spread out his wares and again waited for buyers. After the morning prayers he set his sack in a corner and went from house to house through Goray, examining the mezuzahs, as is the way of packmen, who are generally scribes as well. Whenever he found an error in a mezuzah, he corrected it on the spot with a goose quill, accepted a penny from the householder, and left.

So it went until he came to Rechele's house. The mezuzah on Rechele's doorpost was an old one, covered with a white mold. Reb Itche Mates took a tong from his pocket, pulled out the nails that held the sign to the lintel, unrolled the scroll, and went over to the window for light in which to see whether any of the letters had blurred. It turned out that the word God had been completely erased, and that the right crown was missing from the letter "s" of the name Shaddai. His hands began to tremble, and he said with sternness, "Who lives here?"

"My father lives here—Reb Eleazar Babad," replied Rechele.

"Reb Eleazar Babad," said Reb Itche Mates, and he rubbed his forehead as though attempting to recall something. "Isn't he the head of the community?"

"No longer," Rechele said. "Now he's a rag picker." And she burst into high-pitched laughter.

That a Jewish girl should laugh so unrestrainedly was something new to Reb Itche Mates, and he glanced at her out of the corner of his wide-set eyes, browless and cool green, like those of a fish. Rechele's long braids were undone, like a witch's, full of feathers and straw. One half of her face was red, as though she had been lying on it, the other half was white. She was barefoot, and wore a torn red dress, through which parts of her body shone. In her left hand she held an earthen pot, in her right a straw whisk with ashes in it. Through her disheveled hair a pair of frantic eyes smiled madly at him. It occurred to Itche Mates that there was more here than met the eye.

"Are you a married woman, or a maiden?"

"A maiden," answered Rechele brazenly. "Like Jeptha's daughter, a sacrifice to God!"

The mezuzah fell out of Reb Itche Mates' hand. Never in his whole life, not since he had first stood on his feet, had he heard such talk. His flesh crawled as though he had been touched by icy fingers. He wanted to run away from such sacrilege, but then it came to him that this would not be right. So he sat down on a box and took out a ruler and a bottle of ink. He sharpened his goose quill with a piece of glass, dipped it in the ink, and—wiped it again on his skull cap.

"These are not proper things to say," he told Rechele after some hesitation. "The Blessed Name does not require human sacrifices. A Jewish girl should have a husband and heed the Law."

"Nobody wants me!" Rechele said, and limped so close to him that the female smell of her body overcame him. "Unless Satan will have me!"

She burst into sharp laughter which ended in a gasp. Large gleaming tears fell from her eyes. The pot slipped from her hands and broke into shards. Reb Itche Mates sought to reply, but his tongue had become heavy and dry. The cupboard, the walls, the floor swayed. He began to write, but his hand shook and a drop of ink blotted the parchment. So Reb Itche Mates lowered his head, wrinkled his forehead, and suddenly grasped the secret. For a while, he studied his pale fingernails, and then he muttered to himself:

"This is from Heaven."

❦ 10 ❦

Reb Itche Mates Sends a Proposal

of Marriage to Rechele

Then did Reb Itche Mates the cabalist send messengers to Rechele, enjoining them to speak to her in these words:

The bridegroom is a widower, and a man of no importance. His entire fortune consists of one cotton coat, for both Sabbath and weekday wear; one fringed vest worn on his bare body; one pair of cloth trousers; and one prayer shawl, together with two sets of phylacteries. But the Creator is compassionate and He doth feed all His creatures, from the weasel-

beast to the eggs of the louse. Forty days before Rechele was born it was decreed in Heaven that this
seed, the daughter of Reb Eleazar, was to belong to
Itche Mates. What more is there to say? Let Rechele
agree and the betrothal will take place immediately;
God willing, the groom will give the bridal presents
in the Land of Israel.

The following went to see Rechele: Reb Mordecai
Joseph the cabalist, Levi the rabbi's son, and Nechele
his wife. Reb Mordecai Joseph characteristically
struck his crutch on the floor and admonished Rechele that Reb Itche Mates was a holy man who
fasted from Sabbath to Sabbath, so it would be an
honor to have him as her husband, and the town
where he settled would be protected from evil. Levi
the rabbi's son bit his underlip and fixed his glance
on the girl's face. Dismissing the men, Nechele undertook to arrange matters as one who understood
women. Nechele's shoulders were covered with a
Turkish shawl; she wore a silk kerchief on her head,
as though it were the Sabbath, and two large gold
earrings dangled from her ears. After the fashion of
daughters of good family, her ears had been pierced
many times. Self-importantly she sat down on the
bench used to prepare meat dishes, rested her feet on
a footstool, and motioned the girl to a place opposite
—the bench used for dairy dishes. Then she blew her
nose loudly, wiped her fingers on the voluminous
train of her cloth dress, and spoke as follows:

"Don't put on airs, Rechele, for your father is a

poor man, and has left you in God's care. Besides, you are not well (God save us!). People are already talking and you'll end up in disgrace. Now that you have someone who wants you, let your head be covered and take him. And if it turns out that he doesn't please you, there's always the bill of divorcement."

Then did Rechele, she who was reputed to be half-witted, cover her face with her delicate hands, bend over and begin to cry softly, bewailing her fortune— and she wept as one who has all her wits about her. Her long hair nearly touching the floor, her girlish shoulders quivered. As Nechele spoke the girl sobbed. Her breasts trembled, and she could not utter a word. She was still whimpering when Nechele, who was used to both the screams of women in birth and the shrill mourning of brides, rose and left. A thin smile played about Nechele's lips when she later said to the menfolk: "Ah well, she's not mad at all! Fetch Reb Eleazar home, and she will put on the bonnet soon enough."

Reb Itche Mates' friends collected a few coins and sent a runner to the villages, to locate Reb Eleazar and bring him back. The messenger had been away several days, and there was still no word. People whispered anxiously that both Reb Eleazar and the messenger had been killed in the village of Kotzitza. There was a magician in that hamlet who, it was said, shrank human heads. Meanwhile Reb Itche Mates waited in the dark room in Reb Godel Chasid's home. All day long he sat swaying over the appendix to the Zohar, and working out numerical combinations of the names of Yaweh. At night, when everyone else was asleep, he stole out of Reb Godel Chasid's house and went to the bathhouse, which was situated between the infirmary and the old graveyard. Against the infirmary door rested the purification board awaiting a new corpse. In the moonlight the half-sunken tombstones looked like toadstools. Entering the bathhouse Reb Itche Mates lighted a piece of kindling and held it up like a torch. The walls were black with soot. Cats jumped from bench to bench, silently pursuing each other, with fiery eyes. The scorched stones lay cold and scattered near the oven. Reb Itche Mates took off his clothes. His body was covered with a heavy growth of yellow hair. It was scarred by the thorns and thistles on which he had mortified himself. Silently he went down to the pool by way of the crooked stone steps, noiselessly slipped into the water, submerged himself without a splash, and disappeared for a few minutes. Slowly and cautiously, like some water creature, he lifted his drenched head. Two and seventy times did he immerse himself, according to the numerical signification of the letters Ayin and Beth. When he had done he clothed himself and went off to recite the midnight prayers.

Reb Itche Mates moved restlessly in the room that Reb Godel Chasid had set apart for him, until daybreak. Rather than annoy the mistress of the house, he did not light the wick in the oil lamp. Sprinkling ashes on his head, he strode from wall to wall in the darkness, chanting verses, lamenting the destruction of the Holy Temple, and begging the Holy One, blessed be He, to take back the Divine Presence which he had driven away into Exile with Israel. Between prayers he grew silent, as though attentive to things taking place in other worlds, which his ears alone could discern. Outside the wind blew, rattling shutters and bringing the rending cry of an infant and the singsong lullaby of a mother. Reb Godel Chasid started up from sleep, awoke his wife, and said, "Rechele is greatly honored. Reb Itche Mates is a holy man. She must be righteous too."

They waited for more than eight days, and still there was no word either of Reb Eleazar or the messenger. Every peasant who came to Goray was interrogated:

"Have you heard anything, Ivan, of Reb Eleazar, the owner of the brick house? Or have you perhaps met Leib Banach, who used to buy horses' tails?"

But the peasant would push his sheepskin cap back over his tousled hair, rub his forehead, look far into the distance to jog his memory, blink, and remonstrate: "I've seen nothing, heard nothing. . . ."

And he would stride off in the deep mud.

Thus Goray acquired a new deserted wife and a new orphan. The crows cawed the bad news from the rooftops; Reb Itche Mates was the only one not to be informed of it, for certainly the news would have made him unhappy. The wife of Leib Banach the

Messenger sat for seven days of mourning. Rechele
cried her eyes out and the good women of the town
looked after her. They prepared delicacies for her in
small pots, made over old garments for her to wear,
and came to console her and to talk away the evil spirits. Chinkele the Pious spent the night with Rechele,
that demons might not attach themselves to her.

Rechele was sick. Of the delicacies that were
brought her she tasted almost nothing, and she
missed her period. Hour after hour she moved aim-
lessly about the house like one in a cage, and peered
into every crack and crevice. Sometimes, for no reason, tears began to drop from her eyes, as from a tree
after rain. At other moments she would suddenly fall
to laughing, so loud that the echo resounded through
all the corridors and alcoves of the ruined house. At
night, before going to sleep, she draped the window
of her room with all kinds of old clothes, out of dread
of moonlight. But the bright night spied through the
cracks, light stained the faded walls, trembling in
long pearl strands. Rechele crawled down from bed
in her night dress, listening to the scratching of the
mice and the dry crackle of the firewood behind the
stove. Sometimes a crow outside her window would
awaken with a throaty cry. One day Rechele imagined
that the snowcovered chestnut tree across the way had
begun to blossom.

For a few days Rechele had heard the sound of a
man laughing and braying in the middle of the night.

As often as Chinkele the Pious fell asleep, Rechele would wake her with a tug at the shoulder.

"Chinkele, don't be angry," she would say guiltily. "Somehow, I can't rest."

"Be patient—soon you'll be married to Reb Itche Mates, and nothing bad will come near you," Chinkele would say. "He is a holy man sent by Heaven to save you."

"Chinkele, darling, I'm so afraid of him!" remonstrated Rechele, and her voice broke. "He has dead eyes!"

"You mad creature!" Chinkele cried, infuriated. "God send your enemies such nightmares! Come, lie down near me, and I'll drive off the evil spirit."

Rechele lay near Chinkele, who whispered an incantation. Then Chinkele the Pious began to snore and whistle through her thin nose. Suddenly the old clothes dropped from the window and the room became bright as day. Now Rechele could distinguish everything: pots on the hearth, cobwebs on the walls, and the lions on the eastern wall tapestry, with their heads averted and tongues protruding. One of Chinkele's eyes was half open and glazed, the other shut tight, shrunken as though the liquid had run out of it. There were so many wrinkles in the corners of Chinkele's eyes that she seemed to be laughing in her sleep. Raising herself, Rechele rested her head on her knees, waiting for the cock's crow. Her arms and legs ached, the brains in her skull crumbled like grains of

sand, and thought buzzed about in her head like flies.
Lifting her gaze, she stared into the dazzling snowy
landscape and shuddering, as from many pinpricks,
murmured:

"I've no strength left! Merciful God, take me!"

𝖂 11 𝖂

A Letter from Lublin

An emissary came from Lublin to Goray bearing a
letter for Rabbi Benish Ashkenazi. Written in the
holy tongue, in small ornate characters, with the sig-
nature ending in a flourish, it read thus:

"To the master of the holy teachings, the righteous
one, the foundation of the universe, like unto Joachin
and Boaz, he that is the pillar of our house, for whom
the doors of the fear of the Lord and wisdom are
never shut, the pride of our generation and its glory,
the strong hammer whose learning smashes mountains
and grinds them fine, our rabbi and leader, the man

of God—that is to say, to Rabbi Benish Ashkenazi, may his light shine forever and forever, and may he live many long happy years and in peace, amen.

"I have heard the tidings and pangs and throes assailed me as a woman in labor, and I cried with a loud and bitter cry. For a wicked people have arisen, sons of Belial that did say: 'Let us break the bands asunder and the yoke of the holy teachings and of God (blessed be he!).' And they did trust in the staff of the bruised reed, that sinful man who leads others to sin, like unto Jeroboam the son of Nebath—Sabbatai Zevi is his name, may he be erased from the book of life. Certainly his repute must have reached your ears, for it is many years now since first the cry went forth to all the borders of Judah—that the time of the Messiah was on hand, and that new prophets had arisen, visionaries and stargazers, who were proclaiming: 'In the year 5,426 from the Creation of the World [1665] our redeemer cometh. He shall pass over the river Sambation to the other side. There he shall take for wife the thirteen-year-old daughter of our master Moses. Afterward he shall come back to us riding on a lion, to wage great wars with the peoples of the earth, and to raise up the fallen tabernacle of King David.' I alone, the little one among the thousands of Judah, must confess that I have never inclined an ear or given any credence to this alien talk, which has no sanction in the words of our wise men, of blessed memory, and flows from allusions in the Zohar and other cabalistic volumes, about which I would rather be silent. I shall keep a curb on my mouth, that I may not be burned by their speech, for their bite is as the bite of the fox and their sting is as the sting of the scorpion, and the like. These tidings have brought great confusion to the tents of Israel in Poland, for the wounds we got at the hands of the murderer Chmelnicki (may his name perish!) and from the other cruel men like him, are still festering, and the remnant of Israel is greatly impoverished, and our pride is fallen to the earth—the like has never been seen or heard since the day that Israel was driven from its land. In every town where these tidings came there sprang up empty and lightheaded men that, without considering, accepted the chaff together with the wheat, and let themselves fall into the net which the wicked man had spread at their feet. Likewise a great number of men of wisdom and understanding were captured in that net, or else feared to open their mouths, and cried Amen, despite themselves. Your Honor knows well that a long time must pass before any news can reach our ears from those lands that are under the sceptre of the Turk, and that for the most part there is no substance in such news, wherein truth and falsehood are mingled. Nevertheless, daily new tidings do arrive, filthy and terrifying, which cause our hearts to melt like wax and our knees to grow weak. For witnesses do testify that Sabbatai Zevi doth pronounce the holy name of God, sounding every letter in it, and that he doth make use of the impure names to do his magic and to alter the course of nature, that men may believe in him and his teachings. It is also said that he styles himself in his letters as 'I, your God, Sabbatai Zevi.' Woe to the ears that have heard these things, and woe to the eyes that have seen them! For this is blasphemy and taunting of the Lord, of which it has been said: 'The fires of Gehenna shall be quenched, but their fire shall not be quenched, and they will be an abhorring unto all flesh.' I, the least of men, have sought to search into the roots of the thing—but who can gird his loins against a people that consumes alive all who dare cast the slightest doubt on their depraved belief—this multitude that would not sift pearls from sand? Who knows, perhaps Sabbatai Zevi intends to become the idol of an idolatry, like Mahomet and all the others who have forged the word of God and contaminated the world? If we, the wise men of Poland, the shepherds of our generation, had ourselves but known what he has done and his doings, we might have been able to go forth to meet him, armed with the shafts of the Torah, and we might have waged war upon him, the war of God, until he were utterly destroyed. But, to our sorrow, we know not the man and cannot, until we do, confront him with proof positive; we must in the meantime wait to see what the day will reveal. And though many and great men do err about him, I swear by the living God that Sabbatai Zevi is not our Messiah, for whom our eyes have yearned these nigh two thousand years. For falsehood and deceit drip from his lips. An inciter and a seducer is he, one that hath said: 'I shall devour Jacob and lay waste his habitation,' and of certain he shall meet his downfall. For who then has ever risen against the Eternal One of Israel and prospered? Bitter will be his end, and all the execrations of God in the twenty-sixth chapter of Leviticus and the twenty-eighth chapter of Deuteronomy, and all the curses which Joshua visited on Jericho will certainly fall on his head, Amen, so be His will.

"Nor would I have written all these things, for the time is not yet ripe and we must in the meantime lean upon forgers of letters and spinners of moon-beams (as mentioned above). But by chance the news reached me that there has come to your holy com-munity a man, one Itche Mates by name (as his name is, so is he—Folly his name is, and folly is with him). And this forger and seducer doth give himself out to be a great man, as is the way of all who practice to deceive. He hath made a pit and digged it for young and old, to take them captive through his hypocritical piety and alien ways, the like of which no eye hath ever seen before. From what he says, one is to believe that he fasts from Sabbath to Sabbath, immerses himself many times in the ritual bath (with a rat in his hand!), mortifies his body with all manner of morti-fications—all this he says and does to lead proper peo-ple into error and to seduce them from the path of righteousness, and to cast them into the lowest pit of heresy. Of such men King Solomon, the wisest of all men, hath justly said: 'None that go unto her return, neither do they attain unto the paths of life.' For this man works not through the power of God, but rather through that of the Evil One. He doth work magic. He doth consult with ghosts and his staff declareth unto him, and he hath made a covenant with demons. This has been revealed by the great ones, the kings of the world—and who, say, are the true kings of the world? They are our masters, the rabbis. Every place where the sole of his foot treads, he gives out cures and amulets to heal the sick and drive out evil spirits, like those masters who were able to venture into the vineyards of cabala and emerge unharmed. But those who know cabala truly, those who understand its allusions and mysteries, have searched his amulets closely and have found that he makes use of the names of demons and demonesses, of hobgoblins and brazen hounds (God help and shield us!). And not only have his amulets been of no avail, they have instead brought innocent children, that had not before tasted of sin, as well as pure-hearted men, to die from extraordinary causes, after lingering illnesses. The hair of my flesh doth stand up, for the devils take dominion over those who make use of them, wreaking their vengeance on them both in this world and in the world-to-come. For they attach themselves to the soul and do it all manner of filth. The rabbis, God-fearing and perfect souls, have often warned Itche Mates to cease his practices—for one must warn the culprit before punishing him. But he mocks in his heart the utterances of the righteous. He howls like a

hound with his mouth, and finds a hundred and fifty
arguments with which to declare the unclean clean;
but in secret he clings to Satan and to Lilith, and
offers up sacrifices to them. To demons he doth sacrifice, not to the living God. His pocket is full of forged
letters from the greatest men of the generation, and
his lips drip with deceit. With a tongue of blandish-
ment he doth speak, and the poison is under his gums.
To make matters worse, this false prophet is forever
sunk in melancholy, whose root is lust, as has been
clearly demonstrated by our sages. In every town he
comes to he speaks upon the heart of some woman to
join him in the bond of matrimony, but his purpose
is to make her unclean and to give her a bad name.
For after the marriage his wives all move away from
him, because of his ugly ways; from too much magic
working, he has himself been caught in the web, and
no longer has the strength to act the man's part; he
shall lean upon his house, but it shall not stand. . . .
Nevertheless, he will not divorce them, and lets them
sit alone, grass widows, the tears on their cheeks, their
bitter cries splitting heaven, with no recourse. Woe
to him, and woe to his soul, that shall weep in secret:
Let them curse it that curse the day, who are ready
to rouse up leviathan.

"And now I beg Your Honor, regard not the vessel
but that which is in it, and let this wicked man not
strike root in your holy congregation, whose name is as
ointment poured forth, henna and spikenard. Incline
not your ear to his allusions and falsehoods. Tear him

out by the roots. Beat him, break his head, make him a disgrace and a mockery, and so shalt thou put away the evil from thy midst, as was done with the help of God in other holy congregations. For from the sole of the foot even unto the head there is no soundness in him, but wounds and bruises and festering sores. Tear the veil from his face, to sanctify the name of Him who is on high, and to give the wicked the reward for his wickedness. Let the blood that he has shed fall on his own head. Thou shalt blot out the remembrance of Amalek from under heaven. Drive him off in shame, as have done all the other great men in their towns, and uncover his nakedness for all to see, that he may know that there is a judge and justice in the world, and that Israel is no widower. For the waters are come in even unto the soul, and there is no longer the strength to suffer these hypocrites and prophesyers, who would tear down the branch of Judah—that is, the disciples of the wise—and do away with them utterly. This sheet is too short, and not all things can be said. Give to the wise man and he will be yet wiser, understanding one thing from another. And God shall stand at our side and cleanse the world from the scum of the serpent and the poison of the basilisk. With this I put an end to words and conclude with a broken and a contrite heart, and with faltering knees.

"—From me, who am the smallest of men, the tail of the fox, the threshold to be trodden by the wise. A worm am I, and no man, one to be mocked and despised by all: Jacob, the son of the holy Rabbi Nachum (blessed be the memory of the righteous!), once the head of the holy community of Pintchev, and now resident in the holy community of Lublin (God protect and shield it!)."

❦ 12 ❦

Rabbi Benish Prepares for War

with the Sabbatai Zevi Sect

Rabbi Benish prepared for war with the Sabbatai
Zevi sect. He sent Grunam to search out the packman
Itche Mates and learn his ways, and on the fence of
the prayer house he hung an injunction against reading the tracts from abroad. Rabbi Benish called on
all those who had amulets to bring them in to be
examined, for there were widespread rumors that the
names of impure demons and of Sabbatai Zevi were
written in many of them. On the Sabbath the rabbi
preached in the prayer house between the morning
and the afternoon prayers on the verse in the Song of

Songs: "Awaken not, nor stir up love, until it please"; he pointed out that it was a sin to try to hasten the end of days. Rabbi Benish also told the congregation of the false Messiahs who had risen in days gone by, and of the persecutions that Jews had suffered because of them. To keep the young folk who were cabalists from gathering at midnight as they usually had done, he ordered the study house and the bathhouse closed late at night. Reb Itche Mates was no longer able to immerse himself in the bathhouse before the midnight prayer watch, and was forced to go to the pond beyond the town, taking along a hatchet to chop a hole in the ice. Two young men walked ahead of him with wooden lanterns to light the way, which was full of pits and holes. Reb Itche Mates carried the Book of the Creation to drive off evil spirits. Silently, without a sigh, he took off his clothes, and immersed himself in the water. So as not to lose the small break in the ice, he held on to a rope. After immersion he did not cover his frozen body immediately; instead, he rolled in the snow, recounting his transgressions. He went so far as to beg forgiveness for the pain he had given his mother when he lay in her womb. . . . Rabbi Benish called him a "foolish zealot."

The old rabbi's melancholy mood would not leave him. Ever since the Sabbatai Zevi sect had gained in strength in Goray, he had begun to shout at the members of his household, and had become brusque with the women who asked him ritual questions. He

stopped greeting visitors with "God bless your coming," and avoided prayers with the quorum. His body
stooped as under a heavy load, and he would nap
during the day; this was unusual for him. Waking his
household in the middle of the night, he would de-
mand to have his bed fixed because his body ached
and he was sleepless. With nightfall he ordered the
shutters barred. He wrote many letters that he did
not send, and they were scattered over the table and
the floor. No matter how often his dinner was brought
to him from the kitchen, he would let it grow cold,
until finally it had to be carried off, still untouched.
He no longer reviewed the daily lesson with his students, and, as in times of famine or epidemic, he ordered his bed removed from the bedroom. His face
yellowed and grew wrinkled, and old age overtook
him all at once. Once he sat up all night composing a
will, which he burnt in the oven at dawn. Another
time, calling in ten of his company, he made a declaration to the effect that he remained true to his faith,
and that any statement to the contrary that he should
make before his death should be regarded as lacking
truth and validity. He also wrote this declaration on
parchment with his goose quill, and ordered the witnesses to sign their names to it. For many days afterward the town was full of whispering about this
event, for people did not understand the meaning of
it. Finally, in the Book of the Ford of the Jabbok,
they found a passage explaining that Samael comes
to every dying man with a drawn sword in his hand,

and incites him to deny God; hence, it is best to void any such blasphemy in advance. From this they drew the conclusion that Rabbi Benish was preparing for his end.

Meanwhile, amazing things were taking place in Goray.

It was reported that Mordecai Joseph, the cabalist, was kneading a clay golem in the study house attic, that he might come to the help of the Jews at the birthpangs of the Messiah. Someone saw Mordecai Joseph and a boy haul a sack of clay up the stairs. Of Reb Itche Mates it was said that he experienced an ascent of the soul every night, and that Rabbi Isaac Luria, the holy man, came and revealed the secrets of the cabala to him. Since Reb Itche Mates' arrival in Goray, the Jews of that town had set their hearts on returning to God. The men arose before daybreak to recite psalms, the women fasted Mondays and Thursdays and sent pots of food to the poorhouse. One married woman rapped on the prayer stand one Sabbath and confessed that she had lain with her husband during the days of her impurity. Young newlyweds did not visit their wives on the nights they immersed themselves in the bathhouse. A few select persons gathered every night at Reb Godel Chasid's house, and Reb Itche Mates bared the mysteries of the Torah for them.

On the night of the seventeenth day of Tebet, Rechele was betrothed to Reb Itche Mates; the betrothal

feast took place in the upper floor of Rechele's house.
Benches and tables were set about the room, one section for the men and another section for the women.
At the last moment Rechele changed her mind and
fell to weeping that she did not want Itche Mates. But
she was mollified with sweet talk and gifts until
finally she consented again. Now she sat crowded in
among the women, wearing a silk dress, a kerchief on
her forehead, and a strand of beads that belonged to
Chinkele. Her face was pale, and wry, her large brilliant eyes were full of tears. To divert the bride and
raise her spirits, the women enthusiastically praised
her beauty, stroked her hair, and quickened her with
spoonfuls of moldy citrus preserve. Reb Itche Mates,
in a silk kaftan, sat surrounded by his followers at
the men's table. The oven was stoked, so that the
walls sweated, and the tall candles in the earthen
candlesticks melted so fast that the wicks needed frequent trimming. Reb Itche Mates was in high spirits,
his face flushed, eyes bright. Alluding often to the
mystery of holy sexual union, he expounded new
cabalistic combinations and permutations of holy
letters, while doling out portions of brandy and
spiced wine. So elated did he become that he told the
women to dance, to amuse the bride-to-be. At this
Chinkele the Pious stood up and ordered the table
pushed aside. A Bohemian, she followed that country's customs. The young women mocked her and
guffawed, but Chinkele did not seem to hear them.

Extending her thin arms in their wide, gathered sleeves, she put her small head to one side, circled about and sang in Old Yiddish:

Protect, Lord God, this bride and groom;
May we see the Messiah soon.
The Holy Presence, Lord God, wed
As these two seek the marriage bed.

Ecstatic, Chinkele the Pious wanted them to dance in a circle, but the women were bashful and, crowding around the threshold, they pushed one another forward. Chinkele tried to dance with the bride, but because of Rechele's lameness had to desist. Then, wiping his wet forehead with his sleeve, Itche Mates arose and approached Chinkele. He drew his handkerchief from his breast pocket, held one corner of it, and said to Chinkele, speaking out of the side of his mouth so as not to address her directly: "Take a corner! It is pleasing to the blessed God for us to dance before Him."

Reb Itche Mates pulled up the tails of his kaftan, exposing his white linen trousers and the fringes of his vest, and, covering his eyes with his left hand, he began to scrape his feet. Like a bride at the bridal dance, Chinkele lifted the train of her ruffled satin wedding dress and hopped back and forth in her pointed shoes. The sparkling beads on her bonnet jangled, her hollow cheeks were flushed red, and shining tears dripped from her eyelids. At first everyone looked on in amazement. Some even doubted whether this was not sinful levity. But soon they were silenced, sensing that this dance was not a simple one: great things were transpiring. So profound did the silence become that candle flames could be heard sputtering. Men crowded close together, staring with moist wide-open eyes. A tall, starved-looking young cabalist, with a prominent Adam's apple, swayed violently as though in prayer and, wringing his fingers until the knuckles cracked, he grimaced and squinted. Reb Mordecai Joseph stood in a corner leaning on his crutch. His tousled beard burned, his eyeballs flickered green, torrents of sweat poured down his face, and his whole body jerked spasmodically. For hours on end the two danced without wearying. Their souls seemed to be reaching for the higher spheres. Rechele meanwhile leaned against the edge of a bed, hands covering her face as though she were secretly crying. Suddenly, dragging her lame leg, as though to step forward, she pulled herself up and fell to laughing so violently and so loudly that everyone was startled. Before anyone could reach her, she had fallen and she lay choking with sobs. Her eyes glazed, her arms and legs contorted, foam ran from her twisted mouth. She shuddered, twisted, and a vapor rose from her as from a dying ember.

Reb Itche Mates noticed nothing: the kerchief still in his hand he danced on, his feet stumbled over each other like a drunken man's. His face glowed with mystic enthusiasm, his silk coat was wringing wet; beads of sweat ran down his beard and glided over his open chest. His sash had fallen off, one of his kaftan tails trailed on the drenched floor, his head was turned up and tilted, as though he constantly stared at something beyond the ceiling.

Unable to restrain himself any longer, Reb Mordecai Joseph groaned, pounded the floor with his crutch, and suddenly began to hop about, sobbing and yammering: "Dance, men! Let's not delay! The divine company await us!"

✿ 13 ✿

"The Others" Arrive

It was after midnight. In the bright night that lay over Goray a wind blew, a strong wind that swept away the dry snow and bore it off to pile up in mounds. The frozen earth was bared; trees shook off their winter white; branches broke; moss suddenly appeared on the housetops. In the very middle of the winter the roofs faced the world, with all their rotten shingles and patches. Crows awoke and cawed hoarsely, as at some unexpected sorrow. Snowflakes whirled through the air like wild geese. Between dark, plowed clouds, full of pits and holes, a faceless moon rushed through the sky. One might have thought the town had been doomed to a sudden alteration that had to be completed before the rising of the morning star.

That night Rabbi Benish lay down to sleep later than usual on the bench bed in his study. In his white trousers and prayer vest he lay, resting on three feather-soft pillows, and covered with a comforter. Nevertheless, he could not fall asleep. A whistling and a howling rose from the hearth, and now and then in the stagnant air a sigh as of a soul in torment. The rafter, piled high with ancient holy volumes no longer fit for use, shuddered, and dull thuds were heard from above, as though someone were moving heavy things about. Though the clay oven was stoked, and the windows shut and sealed with braided straw, a cold gust blew through the air, chilling Rabbi Benish's old limbs.

Rabbi Benish attempted to concentrate on Torah as he usually did when sleep had deserted him. But tonight his thoughts ran too rapidly, crowded close on one another, tangled. He pressed his eyelids down over his eyes, but they opened again of their own accord. Half awake and half asleep, his ears caught the sound of speech that seemed to be issuing from many mouths. Several voices were debating stubbornly and hotly. It was the same old everlasting wrangling about Sabbatai Zevi and the end of days that had been running ceaselessly through his mind. Suddenly he started, so violently that his bench bed moved with

him. The voices ceased. In their place there came a
rapping at the rabbi's shutter. He shook himself
awake, sat up, and trembling with fear asked:

"Who's there?"

"It is me, Rabbi. Forgive me."

"Who are you?"

"Grunam."

Rabbi Benish sensed bad news, and his skin prick-
led. After a brief silence he replied, "Just a moment!"

The rabbi crawled out of bed, groped for his
slippers in the dark, and pulled his robe around him.
Then he went to the door. In his confusion he
knocked his head so hard against the top of the doorpost that a lump immediately rose on his forehead.
Blindly, his hand trembling, he lifted the chain,
drew the bolt, and turned the key twice in the keyhole. Grunam burst into the room, bringing the cold
with him, breathing as though someone had been
pursuing him.

"Rabbi," he gasped, "a thousand pardons! A whole
crowd of men and women have gathered together! At
Reb Eleazar Babad's, on the upper floor! Men dancing with women. Profanations!"

Rabbi Benish could not believe his ears. Had
things gone this far in Goray? Without delay and silently he began to dress. In the darkness he found his
trousers, put his fur coat over them, and even located
his broad sash. Several times chairs fell; Rabbi Benish
stumbled against the table edge and hurt himself.
His legs were unusually torpid; a tremor crossed his

back, stabbing icily at his spine. For the first time in
many years Rabbi Benish fell into a fit of coughing.
Old Grunam's eyes shone like those of a cat.

"Rabbi, forgive me," he began again.

"Come," Rabbi Benish almost shouted. "Quick!"

Weak-kneed, Rabbi Benish pulled up his collar. He
expected darkness outside, but it was bright as twi-
light. An icy wind immediately gripped him and took
his breath away. Thin needles of snow or rain—it was
impossible to tell which—began to sting his face,
which immediately swelled. His forehead and eyelids
stiffened and became bloated. Rabbi Benish looked
about him, as though unable to recognize the town,
and wanted to take Grunam's hand, so as not to slip
and fall. But all at once a great hoarse wind rushed
upon him, thrusting him back several steps, and began to drive him downhill from behind. His fur hat,
torn from his head, flew high in the air like a black
bird, crookedly plunged to the earth, and began to
roll madly straight toward the well. Rabbi Benish
seized hold of his skull cap with both hands, and the
ground wavered beneath him.

"Grunam!" Rabbi Benish shouted, in a stranger's
voice.

Later, Rabbi Benish did not know himself how it
had all happened. Grunam began to run after the
sable hat, racing down the steep incline; then, as
though attempting to cover the hat with his body, fell
and rose to fall again. He rolled down the hill and
all at once disappeared entirely, as though carried off.

Casting a terrified glance over his shoulder, Rabbi Benish realized that evil was abroad and tried to return to his house. But at that moment his eyes were filled as with sand. The skull cap fell from his head, the tails of his coat billowed, and began to drag him backward. His head spun and he choked. Suddenly the storm seized him, bore him aloft for a short distance, as on wings, and then cast him down with such violence that in the turmoil he could hear his bones shatter. With the last vestige of his consciousness he was still able to think: "The End."

The whole incident must have taken a few seconds. Grunam arrived in haste with the fur hat, but he could no longer find the rabbi. He was certain that the rabbi had turned back to the house and began to rap on the shutters, calling, but there was no answer. Then, sensing evil, Grunam fell to shouting at the top of his lungs:

"Help, the rabbi! He-lp!"

The first to respond was the rabbi's wife; then his daughters-in-law and grandchildren sprang from sleep. Running outdoors half naked, they roused the town with their frightened cries. At first no one could understand what had happened. Terror had deprived Grunam of speech; instead, he gestured and blinked like a mute. Doors opened on every side. Many of the townspeople feared that marauders had descended on the town, others thought there was a fire. A full half hour passed before Rabbi Benish was found half covered with snow near a chestnut tree some twenty paces from his home. The rabbi's wife fainted when she saw what had happened, and all the women began to lament at once. But Rabbi Benish was not dead. Several men lifted the groaning rabbi and bore him into the study. His face was blue and frozen, his right arm broken or dislocated. One eye was shut, as though pasted together. A vapor rose from his snow-covered beard, and his body shook feverishly. People asked him questions, shouting into his ears, but he did not answer. With difficulty his garments were removed and he was put to bed. The rabbi's lips grew white with the pain, and Ozer's wife moistened them with vinegar. Someone else rubbed the rabbi's temples and blew on his face, to revive him. To brighten the room, one of those who had come running up lighted the braided candle reserved for the Sabbath night ceremony; the candle flickered with a smoky fire.

What had happened soon became known to those at the betrothal feast. Most of the assembled immediately ran off, the women stealing out individually. The candles had already gone out. Only a few damp pine branches low under the tripod spread a flickering glow. The floor was wet, the benches and tables were pushed back and overturned, the ceiling dripped and the smell of brandy and charred embers, as after a fire, hung in the air. Rechele had still not come to, and lay on the bed, damp, her hair wild and her teeth clenched. Chinkele the Pious kept trying to revive her, unbuttoning Rechele's blouse, unclasping hooks, untying laces, pouring juice on her lips and at the same time murmuring affectionately and pleading with her. Reb Itche Mates, his face turned to the wall, stood in a corner, muttering. . . . Reb Mordecai Joseph, who had drunk half a jug full of aqua vitae, jogged Itche Mates' elbow, trying to get him to go home, and, rasping, crowed with pleasure at his foe Benish's downfall.

"Come, Reb Itche Mates. The demons have him now—may his name perish!"

❦ 14 ❦

The Rabbi Forsakes His Congregation

In the study, where Rabbi Benish's canopy bed
had been placed, the oven had been stoked so
high that the plaster was cracking and the heat
scorched. The outside door had been locked to keep
out the cold, and visitors who started coming early in
the morning would pass through several rooms before
entering the one where Rabbi Benish lay. Its floor
was wet and muddy, and it reeked of sickness and
medicines. The citizens of Goray milled about the
sickroom, careworn, chewing at their beards, rubbing
their foreheads, and loudly debating what was to be
done. Women with filthy kerchiefs on their heads

huddled drearily together, whispering in corners, blowing their noses in their aprons, and sighing aloud. The table where the rabbi had studied the Torah for more than half a century had been moved aside; the doors of the bookchest were wide open; the spindly legs of the antique chairs cracked and split under the unaccustomed weight of the visitors, and everything seemed suddenly to be amiss. The sick man lay in his bed under two comforters, his velvet coat on his legs. Perspiration beaded his high, bruised forehead, his eyes were closed, and his beard tangled like flax. His whole appearance had changed.

The rabbi's house was greatly disordered. The rabbi's wife moved about with her head bound and red eyes swollen with crying. Her shoulders stooped even more than usual, her hairy chin kept shaking. She seemed to be constantly muttering something, and in her confusion carried a pot with her wherever she went. The rabbi's daughter—the widow—and his elder daughter-in-law ran to the study house every few hours to supplicate God anew and to light fresh candles. Together, they rushed up the steps leading to the Torah Ark, opened the door to implore the pure Torah scrolls, and cried so piteously that the young men in the study house wept to hear them. Common folk recited psalms, women measured the graves with wicks from which they later made candles to ward off death from the rabbi. Even the rabbi's son Levi, who belonged to the Sabbatai Zevi sect, forgot the differences with his father and joined the other visitors in

the sick room. Only Ozer, the rabbi's eldest, was not
there; he sat in the kitchen, after his fashion, filching
from the pots on the fire food which, in his panicky
haste, he swallowed unchewed. Every now and then
Ozer would come rushing into the sick room with a
sooty face, jostle his way through the crowd, to confusedly ask of all and none: "What's happening? No
better?"

What cures were not attempted! They tried soaking the bad arm in hot water, to soften it, but that
only scorched it. They applied seething salt, but that
made it worse. The keeper of the poorhouse, an expert at nursing the sick, insisted that the arm was
only dislocated, and she tried to snap it back into its
socket, but Rabbi Benish fainted with the pain. His
grandchildren ran from house to house asking for advice, and returned with numerous home remedies:
Honey cakes to apply to the wound, dog fat to smear
on it, malodorous yellow-green salves, mustard plaster.
Two experienced women with headkerchiefs high on
their foreheads, sleeves rolled up, and great aprons
on, stood beside the bed and poured boiling water
constantly from pots into basins, so that the sick
room was dense with steam; they filtered the water
through sieves and lighted glowing coals, as women
do on the eve of Passover when cleansing the Passover
dishes. The room smelled of smoke, charred stones,
and the ritual of the purification of the dead. Whenever anyone asked the sick man how things were with
him, he would open a corner of his eye, look strangely

at his questioner, and instantly sink back into his slumber.

Two messengers had been sent at daybreak to a nearby village to fetch a peasant who was reputedly expert at setting dislocated arms and legs. The messengers were given money and a flask of aqua vitae, and told to drag the peasant by the ears if necessary. They should have returned by now, for the village was barely a mile away. But they were nowhere to be seen. Boys ran outdoors to be on the lookout for the messengers and the peasant. Each of them came back with another reply. Somewhere far away, on a hill, a dot came into sight, but it was uncertain whether it could be the messengers or a sleigh hauling wood. Since the disappearance of Reb Eleazar and Leib Banach, everyone lived in terror. Already the messengers' wives sat with flushed faces in the kitchen of the rabbi's wife, prepared to scream and weep. Eating thickly buttered bread, they sighed like widows. Though it was fiercely cold outdoors, knots of women stood about the market place, hunched in shawls, huddling together and as anxious as though waiting for a funeral. Their feet, thrust into men's great boots, kept up a constant dance. Their faces, prematurely aged, were pale with the frost and the new terror whose shadow was slowly deepening over the town. They all repeated the same refrain:

"It's because of 'the others,' the demons."

"They're the ones to blame."

They gossiped that Nechele, his daughter-in-law,

had bewitched Rabbi Benish. One woman had with her own eyes seen Nechele in secret confabulation with the old witch Kinnegunde. All the women knew for certain that Nechele had a magical elf lock in the chest in her room, and in order to bind her husband, Levi, she would have him drink the water in which she washed her breasts. Glucke, the trustee, swore that, unable to sleep all night, she had heard the noise of women chattering in the wind, and had concluded that the spirits were gathering together. Later, at the very moment when Rabbi Benish was injured, all the spirits had burst into laughter, mocking and clapping their hands—for they had avenged themselves on humans, had done them an injury.

At nightfall the peasant healer finally arrived. The messengers reported that the peasant had refused to come under any circumstance and that they had had to get him dead drunk and drag him all the way. He was a tiny old man, wearing straw shoes and a sheepskin coat with the wool side out. His tremendous hat was pushed authoritatively back over his white curls. His small eyes were red and always smiling. He was led into the room where Rabbi Benish lay; the door was opened wide in his honor, as though he were a great physician. The old man rubbed his hands joyfully together, and began to hee-haw and skip about. His toothless mouth babbled something foolish and sly.

"He wants another cupful," one of the messengers confided to the rabbi's wife.

They poured the peasant half a cup. He took a
piece of dry cheese out of his pocket, bit it, and tears
of pleasure rolled down his cheeks. Then he approached the sick bed to show what he could do. He
looked at Rabbi Benish as though the rabbi were only
pretending to be ill. The moment the peasant grasped
his bad arm Rabbi Benish began screaming and twist-
ing in his bed as though to tear himself free. The
peasant pulled so violently they heard the bone crack.
His drunken face turned blue with the strain and
with sudden wrath. Rabbi Benish gagged and fainted
—they were barely able to revive him. The peasant
fell into a murderous rage and grabbed a vessel and
smashed it to the earth.

"Devils in human shape!" he screamed, and his
fists shook. He seemed to be about to throw himself
at the sick man.

With difficulty they managed to get the peasant
out of the sick room and persuade him to return to
his village. Afraid he might collapse in some field and
freeze to death, he was so drunk—and that the peasants might then accuse the Jews of killing him, and
descend upon the town, they found a man who agreed
to take him home.

Meanwhile, night fell, and, with it came a frost
more bitter than any the old folks could remember.
Water froze in the well, and the pail cracked. An ice
hill formed up to the very rim of the well, and it was
dangerous to go near it, for one false step was enough

to send one over the edge. Though the ovens were heated in every house, small children in their cribs cried with the cold. As always on a night like this, there were numerous accidents and evil afflictions. Infants would suddenly begin to choke, lose their breath, and turn blue. The brandy and pepper placed on their bellies made things even worse. Girls put on men's jackets, bundled up in double layers of shawls, and went seeking women who could avert the evil eye by incantations. In many houses the stoves suddenly began to smoke so heavily that, to avoid suffocation, people had to pour water over the fire. In one house soot began to burn in the chimney, and a ladder had to be quickly found for someone to crawl up the crooked, slippery roof and poke wet sacks and rags down the chimney. Everybody began coughing. Elsewhere, there were cases of frozen arms and legs.

In Rabbi Benish's room the company gradually thinned out, until everyone had left; the room looked like an inn just emptied of guests. Ever since the peasant had tried to push his arm back into its socket, the rabbi's suffering had grown greater every minute. The flesh of his bad arm had swollen, became puffed, and had a fat, ugly smoothness about it; it was steaming with heat. Late at night Rabbi Benish grew delirious with pain. He demanded that his wife pay him in full the one hundred and fifty gold pieces that his father-in-law had pledged. Then suddenly he wanted to know if his dead son-in-law had eaten the evening meal. This was taken as a bad omen, and his family burst into tears. Rabbi Benish opened one eye, came to himself momentarily, and said:

"Take me away to Lublin. For God's sake! I do not want to lie in the graveyard in Goray."

Early the next morning a sleigh with two horses stood before the rabbi's house. Rabbi Benish was dressed and covered with several comforters and whole bundles of straw. Grunam and the rabbi's wife accompanied him. Even his foes gathered and followed the sleigh to the bridge. Women cried and wrung their hands, as at a funeral. One woman flung herself in front of the horses, hoarsely screaming:

"Holy Rabbi, why do you forsake us? Rabbi! Ho-ly Rabbi!"

PART TWO

1

The Wedding

The day of Reb Itche Mates' wedding. For three
days, engaged in a constant round of mortifications,
he had not taken so much as a spoonful of warm
water into his mouth. Nights, without removing his
clothes, he sat with his feet in a bucket of cold water
to keep him awake and mumbled perpetually. For
days on end he strayed somewhere in the hills, sinking to his knees in the snow, as though he sought for
someone in the white, luminous fields. The cold
baths had made his voice hoarse; his eyes were
overcast and extinguished like a blind man's. On his

wedding day he lay on the bench in his small room in
Reb Godel Chasid's house, surrounded by the faithful, who attended his every word. There was even
one young cabalist who wrote down whatever Reb
Itche Mates said. —The women devoted themselves
to Rechele.

Ever since Itche Mates had, as a groom-to-be, been
called to the pulpit to read out of the Torah scroll the
Sabbath before the wedding, Rechele had shown no
further signs of rebellion. She listened submissively
to the older women's instructions. She was already
versed in the laws dealing with a wife's cleanliness
and had read through all the women's books concerning purity and modesty. On her pale cheeks two
red spots had settled and would not vanish. Chinkele
the Pious daily for hours on end instructed Rechele
in morality, stroked her head, and kissed her with
cold lips, as though Rechele were her own daughter.
The previous evening, Rechele had been taken to the
bathhouse for the first time. As they always did at a
virgin's first visit, the bandsmen followed her, playing a merry dance tune. A number of women accompanied Rechele, forming a circle around her that she
might not be contaminated by encountering a dog or
a pig on the way. Vulgar street boys shouted lewd words
and obscenities after her. In the bathhouse Yite the
Attendant took charge of Rechele, undressed her, and
felt her loins and breasts to determine whether she
might be barren. With great care, Yite cut the nails
of Rechele's hands and feet, so that there might be no

barrier to the water at Rechele's immersion, combed
her long hair with a wooden comb, and scrutinized
all the unseen places of Rechele's body for an abscess
or horny skin. Women with shaven heads or badly
shorn hair, veteran bathers, sauntered comfortably
about, perfectly at home; stark naked, with breasts
hanging like lumps of dough, with mighty hips, and
loose bellies from continually carrying and giving
birth. Waddling about, they familiarly splashed their
feet in the puddles of water on the stone floor and
diligently tended to the abashed Rechele: they gave
her advice on how to arouse her husband's desire
and taught her what luck-charms to use to conceive
male children. The very young women, with their
small sheep's heads, played in the bathhouse like
silly children, touching Rechele's unshorn hair in
amazement, chasing one another about, and being
generally frivolous. In a corner of the bathhouse the
healer tapped veins, set leeches, and fastened sucking
cups. The floor was as bloody as a slaughter house.
An elderly woman spoke grossly to Rechele and confided things to the girl's ears that sent the blood
rushing to her head, and she almost sank to the earth
with humiliation.

It was the day of the wedding. Rechele sat on a
chair, her feet resting on a footstool, and read a book.
She was fasting that day, and in the afternoon would
recite the Yom Kippur confession, since all one's sins
were forgiven on one's wedding day, as they were on
Yom Kippur. Her thin lips were white; her eyes

gazed into the distance. Her face was livid and drawn as after a long illness. In the house two cooks busily baked white bread and honey cake, cut out cookie dough, dipped feather brushes in oil and egg yolks, poured honey, and crushed almonds in a pestle. Fish and meat had been fetched from a neighboring town. The great pots steamed, and the women kept removing the scum with wooden ladles and trying the broth, to make sure it was tasty. They had baked a long white bread and braided its two narrow tapering ends; holding this loaf they would dance to meet the bride and groom after the ceremony; it was decorated with various good luck tokens: ladders, birds, wheels. Seamstresses sat on the bed putting the last touches to the white satin bridal dress and underclothes. The needles flashed between their much-pricked fingers. Their glances were lowered to their work but their genteel mouths smiled incessantly and grimaced at the constant gossip of the eldest of them, a widow. Everywhere were long sheets with red tooth-shaped fringes on the hems, embroidered pillow cases, and lace-edged underclothes. The new linens crackled in the women's hands, and dazzled the eyes, like the snow outside the window. The house smelled of cinnamon, raisins, and preparation for the feast that ends a fast.

In the evening the girls began to congregate at Rechele's house. The floor was sprinkled with yellow sand, and a few tallow candles were burning. The healer and his son, strumming on their fiddles, were paid in paper pennies for each number. Rechele sat in her bride's chair, wearing a white satin dress and borrowed jewelry. Around her neck hung a thick gold chain. From her pierced ear lobes dangled two long earrings, black with age, their stones clouded. Two girls who were still almost children sat on either side of Rechele. They were to be her bridesmaids, and it was their duty to remain at her side and to protect her. Since no wedding jester could be found in Goray, this role was taken by Doodie, a poor shoemaker blind in one eye. Frightened and pale, he stood at the door, hoarsely and mechanically reciting phrases in Yiddish, his manner so ambiguous it was impossible to tell whether he wished to make people merry or sad. His good eye remained fixed; the one with the tumor kept blinking rapidly. Doodie imitated women crying; he covered his face with dirty hands and bleated like a goat. The girls nudged one another and giggled. They performed first the Mad Dance and then the Scissors Dance and the Water Dance, lifting their dresses as though to cross a puddle. Like strangers they averted their eyes. It was some time before they agreed to accept the pieces of honey cake which were their due; they tasted only a single berry of the jam set before them. Because the fool did not jest, some of the girls upbraided him; others flirted with the player, who wore an effeminate jacket and a plush hat with earlaps, and who kept making vulgar comments under his breath. The girls scolded him, surreptitiously shaking their fingers at him, convulsing with laughter.

"The rascal!" they cried, falling into one another's arms.

Rechele covered her eyes with a handkerchief, remembering her father, Reb Eleazar Babad, who had been killed on the road and had not even been buried in a Jewish grave. Remorse consumed her; she had been unable to visit her mother's grave in Velodova and as was proper invite her to the wedding. Suddenly the women crowded together. The menfolk approached, accompanying the groom who came to cover the bride's head. They could be heard already on the stairs, and the girls tried to lock the door against them. But the door was forcibly pushed open and the men entered, drunk and in high spirits. They soon filled the house. Elbowing the women aside, so that Reb Itche Mates might not have to pass among them, his companions made a path for him, crying haughtily, "Women, to one side! Let us through! Girls—go home!"

As is the custom at weddings, when frivolity is tolerated, a few young women screamed. Reb Itche Mates entered, in a borrowed fur coat which dragged behind him on the floor and wearing a sable hat that fell over his eyes. Before covering the bride's head he recited an interminable prayer. Rechele cried out only once. When Itche Mates covered her head, a rain of raisins and almonds fell on her, and all the

women sobbed and blew their noses. The fool stood
on tiptoe at the door so as to be seen, despite his
smallness, and chanted in a melancholy way:

"The haidamaks *slaughtered and martyred us.*
They murdered young children, they ravished
women.
Chmelnicki slit open bellies, he sewed cats in-
side, (because of our sins!).
This is why we wail so loudly and implore
Revenge, O Lord, the blood of thy slaughtered
saints!"

A woman suddenly fainted, and they poured water
over her. A boy suffocating in the crowd screamed in
fright. Someone stumbled over the water tun. A vessel broke. And then the groom was escorted to the
bridal canopy, which stood between the prayer house
and the old cemetery. Small mounds filled the prayer
house court, marking the graves of school children
who in 1648 had died martyrs' deaths at the hands of
haidamaks and Tartars rather than change their
faith and be sold into slavery. The groom, in memory of the day of death, put on a white robe like a
shroud and a white mitre. He had sprinkled with
ashes the spot on his forehead where the phylacteries
usually rested. Hunched under the canopy Reb Itche
Mates hid his eyes with a kerchief. The four men who
were holding the canopy poles shuffled their feet to
keep warm and blew on their hands. Mischievously
an urchin thrust his grandmother's knitting needle

into the groom's buttocks. The groom did not so much as move, and the boy's arms fell to his side. For a long time all were still. Fragments of ancient monuments loomed above the decrepit fence surrounding the cemetery; in serried ranks they rose above one another. Then suddenly the red leaping flames of braided candles approached, and all became merry. To the tune of a bridal canopy march played by the healer and his son, the bride was led forth. Girls in white, bearing wax candles, formed two rows through which Rechele passed. Completely veiled, she limped more markedly than usual; the bridesmaids almost had to drag her. Levi, Reb Benish's younger son, he that belonged to the Sabbatai Zevi sect, was the master of the sacrament. Pale with the fear of punishment that he, not Ozer, was filling his father's place, the narrow glass in his hand trembled, and the wine spilled over his fingers, as he chanted tearfully:

"Blessed art thou, O Lord, who has sanctified us by thy commandments . . . who has sanctioned unto us such as are wedded to us by the rite of the canopy and the sanctification. . . . Blessed art thou, O Lord, creator of men."

☙ 2 ☙

The Seven Days of Benediction

It was now three nights since they had led the bride and groom to the marriage bed, and Rechele was still a maiden. Early each morning, after Reb Itche Mates had left for the study house, the two women who had given the bride away came, along with a few other interested matrons, to discover whether Rechele and her husband had as yet known each other. Ashamed, Rechele hid under the bolster, but that did not bother them, for was she not an orphan, with no mother to look after her? And so they uncovered her, and examined her slip and bedclothes carefully, their faces reddening as they piously went about their work. Each day they would ask the same question: "Well, have you been together? Has he lain with you?"

The crows were already proclaiming the news from the rooftops to the amusement of the frivolous in Goray. As for Reb Itche Mates, he began to pray behind the oven in the study, hiding his face in his prayer shawl, so that his devotions might not be disturbed by the grimaces of ruffians and apprentices. The followers of Sabbatai Zevi saw that measures had to be taken and Reb Godel Chasid brought Itche Mates home with him for the express purpose of feeding him roasted garlic and saltless peas, food that would make a man potent. Rechele also received instruction, Nechele explaining to her the ways of arousing lust in a husband. And for seven nights, as was the custom, bride and groom were led to the marriage chamber and all waited expectantly for the consummation. During this period, the time of the Seven Benedictions, all the members of the sect gathered together at the evening meal. Rechele still wore her white bridal canopy dress and jewelry, for she was still a bride. She sat shyly on her chair while the shoemaker passed lewd remarks to rouse everyone's spirits. Reb Itche Mates wore a coat of satin. His forehead was flushed, and he was forever wiping the perspiration from his face with his pocket handkerchief. He scarcely touched the dishes set before him, and what he did eat he swallowed with revulsion. The food seemed to stick in his throat. When the subject of marital relations came up he would shake his head, his dead eyes blinking in terror.

"Yes . . . yes . . . of course," he would stammer.

In the afternoons young men were despatched to Reb Itche Mates, grooms who were still boarding at their in-laws', to keep him occupied and prevent him from being melancholy. They asked each other riddles, played at Goats and Wolves, chess, and even dice. Some of them wrote in a fine, curlicued script to exhibit their learning; others kneaded soft bread into all kinds of birds and beasts. Those who could sing did so, and the bright ones thought up new turns of *pilpul*. A few young men who were students of world affairs conversed about the ancient wars of which they had read in Josephus, as well as about the remarkable behavior of rich lords and knights and of the Polish nobleman Wisniewcki, the friend of the Jews, who had impaled the *haidamaks* on wooden poles. They enjoyed discussing the great fairs in Lublin, where the rarest volumes and manuscripts, precious gold and silver objects could be purchased, and where the wealthiest men from Poland, Lithuania, Germany, and Bohemia sought husbands for their daughters. One of the young men even brought his fiddle along with him and played him Wallachian melodies. Amongst them Reb Itche Mates sat, weary and alien, gazing obliquely over their heads. Occasionally he would pull a hair from his beard, hold it close to his eye, stare at it long, and finally place it carefully between the leaves

of the Zohar. Soon his head sank on his chest and he
dozed off. His arms dangled limply and his nose
looked pale and lifeless. His visitors stood up and
chuckled behind his back. At night, when the important leaders of his sect came to escort Reb Itche
Mates to bed, they took him aside for a whispered
conference, remonstrating:

"How can this be, Reb Itche Mates? To be fruitful
and to multiply is the principle of principles!"

The marriage bed was in a room in Reb Eleazar's
half-ruined brick house. Before removing his clothes
Reb Itche Mates read the prayers of Rabbi Judah
the Devout for more than an hour. Next, beating his
breast with his thin fist, and weeping, he made his
confession. Then he walked innumerable times
around a bench. Rechele lay in bed waiting for him,
prepared to greet him with sweet talk and love, as
she had been tutored by the women. Outside, dogs
howled mournfully, grew silent, and then began
again, as though lamenting some great crime perpetrated on them. Rechele became aware that the
Angel of Death was outside. The wind tore at the
shutters, icily swept through the room, and the tallow
candle flickered and went out, leaving the room dark
and smoky. Reb Itche Mates continued his chant as
he shuffled from corner to corner, as though in search
of something. It seemed to Rechele that there was
someone besides Reb Itche Mates in the room, some
airy and terrifying presence. The roots of her hair
tingled with fear, and she drew the covers over her.

At last, silently, Reb Itche Mates lay down beside her. His body smelled of bathhouse water and corpses. He warmed his frigid hands between her breasts, and his bristly hair pricked her, yet his teeth continued to chatter and his body shook so that the bed shook with it. Reb Itche Mates' knees were bony and sharp and seemed to be hollow; his ribs protruded like barrel staves. All at once he spoke, in a low hoarse voice full of childish mystery:

"Do you see anything, Rechele?"

"No! What do you see, Itche Mates?"

"Lilith!" Reb Itche Mates cried, and it seemed to Rechele that the vision pleased him. "Look at her. Long hair like yours. Naked. Concupiscent."

He rambled on in strange half-sentences, cryptic, incomprehensible, as though in mockery. Suddenly he began to snore, with a long, shrill whistle.

"Itche Mates!" Rechele called in a voice which though muffled had a threat in it.

"Eh . . . ?"

"Are you asleep?"

"Uh. . . ."

"Why do you snore so loudly?" asked Rechele.

Itche Mates listened, yet the snores continued even though he was awake.

Rechele was terrified.

"Itche Mates!" she cried, turning from him. "I am sick. Stop frightening me!"

He could not sleep all night. He left the bed and began washing his hands and splashing water on the floor, while muttering prayers and humming. Toward dawn he stationed himself at the window and peered through the cracks in the shutters for sign of light. At the first hint of blue, he put on his clothes and left the house. Only then did Rechele sleep. Tormented by dreams, she saw her father lying in a field, empty-eyed and circled by a flock of vultures. Uncle Reb Zeydel Ber came to Rechele also. He was wearing a bloody shroud, and he waved a long butcher's knife in the air, and shouted angrily: "Your days are numbered! Descend, Rechele, descend into the dark grave!"

She rose in the morning altered, as though by a mysterious disease, and it seemed to Rechele that the night had been longer than nights usually were. She could on no account remember what she had dreamed and what she had experienced. Her head was heavy; her hair hurt, as though it had been pulled; there were blue circles under her eyes, and her body was black and blue as though it had been pinched. Stiffly she walked to the oven and rubbed the flints together until the wick at last caught fire. Then she put a pot on the tripod, but so forgetful was she that the food burned. Reb Itche Mates returned from the study house at noon, wearing a kerchief around his loins and stooping as he carried a great prayer bag. Selecting some dry bread from the kneading trough, he washed his hands and wiped them on the tail of his kaftan. First he dipped the small piece of bread in salt, then shook off some of the salt and dipped the bread again—thus three times. Afterward he rubbed a clove of garlic into the crust. After the meal, he leaned his forehead on the corner of the table, and dozed for a quarter hour. Occasionally his shoulders would jerk. Suddenly he wrenched himself from sleep. There was a red mark on his forehead, and his eyes stared confusedly. Rechele spoke to him, but he seemed unaware of her presence, and did not respond. Presently he stood up, kissed the doorpost sign three times, and went off again—until evening. . . .

When the seventh day of the Seven Days of the Marriage Feast was passed, Rechele was still a virgin. Young women who spoke of it in the shops pitied Rechele who, they said, had had "her head cut off with no knife." Everyone believed that sorcery had prevented the bride and groom from consummating their marriage. The fringes of Rechele's shawl were searched for knots, and the folds of her dress for hidden evidence of witchcraft. All the brooms were taken from her house and burned. The bridal bedding was smoked out and amulets were hung in every corner, to drive off evil spirits. Led separately to the bath, Red Itche Mates was examined by the men for signs of maleness. . . .

And the good-for-nothings who sat in the tavern making fun of law and order had found a nickname for Reb Itche Mates. They called him Gelding.

3

Reb Gedaliya

Some time before the Feast of Purim there arrived in
Goray an emissary with amazing, if bewildering,
news.

Sabbatai Zevi—he related—having already, with
God's help, been revealed as the Messiah, had departed for Stamboul to claim the crown of the Sultan
who ruled the Land of Israel. Not through the might
of hosts had Sabbatai Zevi conquered, but through
the power of lords and prophets from the other side
of the River Samation who accompanied him riding
on the backs of elephants, leopards, and water oxen.

Sabbatai Zevi himself (may his name be praised!)
rode before them on a wild lion, wearing garments
of purple and spun gold and numerous precious
stones that shone in the darkness. A sash of pearls girdled his loins. His right hand clasped a scepter, and
he was fragrant as the Garden of Eden. The sea
parted before him, as it had in days of old for our
Master Moses (peace be with him!), and he walked
upon dry land in the midst of the waters, he and
those that were with him. A pillar of fire went before
him to show the way, and angels flew after him, singing hymns in his praise. At first the kings and princes
of the earth had dispatched hosts of giants with
drawn swords against Sabbatai Zevi, that they might
take him prisoner. But a torrent of great stones
rained from heaven as had been promised for the day
of Gog and Magog, and all the giants perished. The
world was astounded. The people of Judea were now
in high repute. Princes and kings came to honor them
and prostrated themselves before them. Earth and
Heaven would rejoice on the day that Sabbatai Zevi
arrived in Stamboul. All the Jews would certainly
celebrate the Feast of Weeks in the Land of Israel.
The Holy Temple would be restored, the Tables of
the Law returned to the Holy Ark, and a High Priest
would enter the Holy of Holies. Sabbatai Zevi, the
redeemer, would reign throughout the world. . . .

The bearer of this news was no common person, no
ordinary traveler, but Reb Gedaliya, the ritual slaughterer from Zamość, a man who was held in high re-

gard, an individual of standing; Reb Gedaliya was tall,
heavyset, with a great belly and creases in his neck. His
coat was of beaver and covered with silk, and the hat
he wore was sable. His black, broad, fan-shaped beard
hung down to his waist, his curly hair fell over his
shoulders. Reb Gedaliya's name was well known to
the Sabbatai Zevi sect, for he was renowned as a cabalist; it was because of his belief in Sabbatai Zevi that he
had been forced to leave his native town. Reb Gedaliya had come to Goray to rally the believers—perhaps also to take over the office of slaughterer which
had been vacant in Goray since 1648. Beasts and
fowls could be purchased cheaply in the nearby villages, and all the people of Goray longed for meat.
Levi, who now occupied the rabbinic chair in his late
father's place, led Reb Gedaliya respectfully into the
study house, seated him at the eastern wall, and summoned his sect to a feast in honor of the famous man.
The tavern-keeper, who was one of the brotherhood,
brought a cask of sour wine that had lain in his cellar
for more than fifty years, and Nechele set out cookies,
butternuts, and preserves. The guests sang hymns of
the new Messiah which he himself had heard in para-
dise. Reb Gedaliya skillfully poured wine for himself
into a tall silver beaker, thrust his huge hairy hands
into his embroidered sash, and enumerated the many
joyful happenings.

He related how on the great German Sea Jews and
Christians alike had seen a ship whose sails and
ropes were of white silk. The sailors spoke in the holy

tongue, and on the ship's flag were inscribed the words: "The Twelve Tribes of Israel." In Izmir, three days in succession, a voice from Heaven had cried: "Touch not my messiah Sabbatai Zevi!" The Fast of the Tenth of Tebet had been turned into a holiday, into a day of rejoicing. Wherever the testament of the Messiah came, there men ate meat, drank wine, and blew the ram's horn. In the great communities of Hamburg, Amsterdam, and Prague, all the Jews— men and women alike—danced in the streets, holding the Torah scrolls, adorned with crowns and precious stones. Bandsmen played, beat on drums, rang bells, and carried a white canopy before them. On the Sabbath the priests blessed the congregations, as in the ancient days when the Holy Temple was still standing, and thrice daily the cantor led the congregation in the psalm beginning, "O Lord, in Thy strength the king rejoiceth." In every land new prophets were appearing. Ordinary men—even girls and Christians—were throwing themselves to the earth and crying aloud that Sabbatai Zevi, the anointed of the Lord (blessed be He!), had come to redeem God's elect, the Children of Israel. Sinners who until then had openly denied and angered God, had now become penitent, putting on sackcloth and wandering from town to town in atonement and calling upon the multitudes to confess their sins. Rich converts were discarding their wealth and prostrating themselves at the feet of the rabbis, pleading to be readmitted into the fold. Jerusalem was being rebuilt, and rose once more in all her former splendor. In many towns death had become unknown.

Reb Gedaliya said many other things, and the more he said the more flushed the faces of his listeners became, and the more crowded and festive it grew in the house. Nechele and the other women who were serving the guest of honor shed tears of joy and embraced one another. The men listened intently so as not to miss a word. They stood shoulder to shoulder, muttering to themselves and trembling at the thought of the great days that were coming. Reb Godel Chasid sought to elbow his way through the crowd so that he might look Reb Gedaliya in the face but was swept off his feet. A boy fainted and had to be carried into the open air. The eyes of the young men were alight with holy enthusiasm, their ear locks shook, and beads of sweat ran down their foreheads. Although Levi had gone to great lengths to see that there should be no commotion at the feast and that only those who were members of the sect should be present, the people of Goray had heard of the arrival of the newcomer. Boys and girls besieged the windows of the study house, people trampled one another in their eagerness to hear the stranger's message. Reb Gedaliya placed his arms on the shoulders of two young men, climbed on the table, and turned toward the door where the crowd had gathered. His robust figure and sympathetic words won them over immediately.

"Don't push, brothers!" he cried, in a kind, fatherly

voice. "I am staying with you. If God wills it, we shall rejoice often."

Life seemed to have become more pleasant in Goray with Reb Gedaliya's appearance. Despite the frost, the day was sun-filled. The snowy hills around Goray reflected sunlight, blinding the eyes, and miraculously blending earth with sky. The air smelled of Passover, of salvation, and of consolation. Hearing that a slaughterer had arrived in town, the village runners lost no time in setting out for the nearby villages to purchase calves and fowl. Next morning the town resounded to the mooing of cows, the cackling of geese, and the crowing of hens. Broths and roasts appeared once more. Out of their old pantries the women drew moldy salting boards and soaking vessels, skimming ladles and chop knives. Once more they gathered about the cloven butcher blocks, which had been unused and abandoned for many years; butchers stood amongst them splitting marrow bones with sharp hatchets, and carving out the lungs, liver, and intestines. A bloody hide already hung on a fence, to dry in the wind. Even the gentiles were pleased, for now the fat backsides and tallow could be bought cheaply. In the study house, where Reb Gedaliya came to pray the third day after his arrival, it was discovered that he did not recite prayers but sang them. Three gold crowns decorated his Turkish prayer shawl; his skull cap was silver-stitched like those worn on Yom Kippur. His snuff box was of bone, his pipe had an amber head, and a silver pouch held his tobacco. He pinched all the boys' cheeks lovingly and praised them to their fathers. For the scholars he had learned explications; ordinary people were delighted with his witticisms. After the prayers he sent out for a quart òf whiskey and a honey cake. He sliced the cake himself with his small knife, which had a mother-of-pearl handle, and dealt the slices out to each one according to his years and situation, calling them all by name, and forgetting no one. Extending his full, warm hand, he wished each "to meet soon, in Jerusalem, at the gate of the Holy Temple."

Reb Gedaliya was a welcome newcomer to the citizens of Goray, and he revived their declining spirits. His arrival was a sign that the town would rise again. The Sabbatai Zevi sect led by Levi immediately forgot the melancholy Itche Mates, and entrusted their leadership to Reb Gedaliya. Nechele, the rabbi's wife, praised him in the women's section of the prayer house, and bade the women send him Sabbath puddings. Even the old conservative citizens of Goray, the opponents of Sabbatai Zevi, did not openly step forth against Reb Gedaliya; because they too relished a spoonful of broth and a bit of meat, they pretended neither to see nor hear. Reb Mordecai Joseph rapped his crutch on the study house floor, flourished his left fist, and shouted:

"Reb Gedaliya is a holy man! A righteous man! and the righteous endure forever!"

❦ 4 ❦

The Rejoicing in Goray

Reb Gedaliya performed wonders. In every house his wisdom and talents were discussed. He had brought a kerchief with him on which the name of Sabbatai Zevi was stitched. When it was placed on the bellies of women in travail, their birth pangs ceased immediately. From the saintly Rabbi Michael of Nemerov he had brought magic pearls and coins worn smooth by many fingers. He knew how to make ointments for scaldhead and pills to prevent excessive menstruation. Since coming to Goray, Reb Gedaliya had saved many a soul. With his amulets

he exorcised evil spirits from a house where they had
dwelt and multiplied for years; he also restored the
power of speech to a child who had been frightened
by a black dog. Reb Gedaliya's piety and learning
were famous.

Levi was still young, unaccustomed to the yoke of
a congregation, and Reb Gedaliya became the true
leader of Goray. He ruled on all the difficult cases,
and occupied himself with ministering to the spiritual needs of the community. With Levi he visited the
mill, to pronounce it fit to grind the Passover wheat,
examined specimens of the grain, and went from
house to house with a bag to collect for the poor.
Never since Goray first became a town had the rich
given so much to the poor. Reb Gedaliya completely
overwhelmed the wealthy with his smooth tongue,
and enchanted them with his grand manner. Two
weeks before the holiday the people of Goray began
to bake unleavened bread. Reb Gedaliya himself
drew from the well the first bucket of water that
would be allowed to settle overnight; he taught the
kneaders how to knead properly, the water pourers
how to pour, the hole punchers how to punch holes.
He even rolled up his coat sleeves, and, covered with
flour, stood at the table beside the women. He even
shoved the unleavened bread into the oven with the
long wooden paddle. Not, like Rabbi Benish, with
wrath and harshness, did Reb Gedaliya oversee the
preparation of the matzoth, but with rejoicing and
blandishments. With a long pipe constantly between

his fleshy lips he watched everything that went on.
The older women heaped blessings on him and said
the Divine Presence was upon him. The young
women and girls blushed and became more diligent.
Smiling, Reb Gedaliya showed a mouth full of strong
yellow teeth, and cried:

"Hurry, children! Next year we shall eat matzoth
in the Land of Israel! The angels will prepare it!"

On the Great Sabbath before Passover, after Levi's
explication, Reb Gedaliya preached a sermon that
was full of admonitions and consolations. He reminded the congregation that the days of exile were
numbered, and warned them that the last souls who
were to be brought into the world waited beneath the
Throne of Glory. He scolded them that so many
young men and girls were still unmarried. Such neg-
lect of the principle of fruitfulness would delay
their redemption. He demonstrated by means of
cabala that all the laws in the Torah and the
Shulchan Aruch referred to the commandment to be
fruitful and multiply; and that, when the end of days
was come, not only would Rabbi Gershom's ban on
polygamy become null and void, but all the strict
"Thou shalt nots," as well. Every pious woman
would then be as fair as Abigail, and there would be
no monthly flow of blood at all; for impure blood
comes from the Evil One. Men would be permitted
to know strange women. Such encounters might even
be considered a religious duty; for each time a
man and a woman unite they form a mystical com-

bination and promote a union between the Holy
One, blessed be He, and the Divine Presence. Reb
Gedaliya explained all these things in a pleasant way
and with many parables; he recited from memory
whole sections from the Zohar and other works of
cabala and adorned his speech with mystical combinations and permutations. Several times he raised
his glance to the women's gallery, which was fuller
than it had been in former years. It was well known
that the women looked on Reb Gedaliya with sympathetic eyes.

A few days before Passover the village runners
brought a great abundance of beasts and fowls into
Goray. These could be purchased for very little, and
Reb Gedaliya had requested that no expense be
spared, for the coming Passover would be the final
one before the redemption. From early morning until
late at night he stood before a blood-filled pit and,
with his long butcher's knife, tirelessly cut into warm,
distended necks, slaughtering innumerable calves
and sheep, hens, geese, and ducks. The month of
Nisan arrived, mild and sunny. From the hills
around Goray the last traces of snow disappeared.
The long, deep gutters that extended through the
town to the river overflowed, flooding all inclines
and even the floors of houses. The puddles mirrored
bits of sky; rippled by the slightest breeze, they grew
turbid, like deep waters. School boys ran barefoot.
The peasant women coming to Goray to sell eggs
and horseradish, lifted their dresses high, and

splashed about with naked feet. Here and there the first grasses sprouted. A tumultuous throng filled the courtyard where Reb Gedaliya was slaughtering. Sooty housewives and daughters, with their sleeves rolled up, were scrubbing tables and benches in honor of the holiday, scouring them with ashes, scraping so fiercely with their knives that the noise grated. Boiling water in a kettle, they cleansed the crockery and cutlery. With bare, scorched fingers they carried glowing coals and threw them into the hissing water. Reb Gedaliya was surrounded by a dense crowd of women and girls. The feathers flew above his head, like snow, and were borne off in clouds of steam. The women pushed and quarreled among themselves. From every side hands were raised, clutching pent fowl. Wings fluttered and beat, blood spurted, smearing faces and dresses. Bent over the stump of an old tree, Reb Gedaliya accepted pennies with accustomed speed and constantly joked, for he hated sadness, and his way of serving God was through joy.

His Seder was held in the study house, where he was joined by the rest of the Sabbatai Zevi sect. Seated at the head of the table, he wore a white smock, a high mitre on his head; his beard and ear locks were combed and moist from the bathhouse. The candle flames were reflected in the gold-stitched skull caps, in the satin seams of the sleeves, in the polished and gilded wine glasses, and in the women's jewelry. The women sat with the menfolk,

as Reb Gedaliya had bidden. They mingled the unleavened bread with the meats, the dumplings with
the pancakes, and all ate and drank together, like
one family. Reb Gedaliya, who was a widower, having buried his fourth wife, leaned back at his ease
on his pillowed chair and bade all the boys ask the
Four Questions together; further, he permitted more
than the prescribed four goblets of wine to be drunk.
Among those at the Seder in the study house were
Reb Itche Mates and his wife Rechele. Reb Gedaliya
seated Rechele at his right hand, and he told her of
the Messiah's wife, Sarah, who dazzled kings with her
loveliness. He informed her in confidence that Sarah
had once been an inmate of a brothel in Rome. He
addressed Rechele courteously as though she were
one of the sect.

"Rechele," he said, "the angels and seraphim are
envious of your noble spirit. The root of your name
is Rachel, and Rachel's beauty is yours."

From that night on there was no end to the rejoicing in Goray.

Both the first and the second days of Passover
each man who went to the dais to recite his blessing
of the Torah was required to add a special blessing
for Sabbatai Zevi, and the cantor chanted:

"May He who bringeth aid to His kingdom, bless
and guard, assist and exalt, glorify and raise on
high, our Master, the holy rabbi and saint in whom
we are saved, Sabbatai Zevi, the Messiah of the God
of Jacob."

Between the morning and afternoon prayers Reb Gedaliya in his sermon commanded the people of Goray to clear the dogs, cats, and other unclean beasts out of their homes. The afternoon following the feast there was dancing in the courtyard of the prayer house, men and women circling together. Schoolboys leaped like goats and sang: "The white doves preen —The Messiah has been seen!" Powerful men carried the lame Reb Mordecai Joseph on their shoulders; young men whirled this way and that and engaged in all sorts of nonsense. Even gentiles came to watch the Jews amuse themselves. During the intermediate days of the holiday, marriage contracts were written and good-luck plates were broken in every house where there was a girl over eight. Shortly after Passover new tales of Sabbatai Zevi's prowess circulated in Goray.

It was said the Turks in Stamboul had attempted to rise against Sabbatai Zevi, and he had taken refuge in a fortress set aside for him since the Six Days of Creation, after killing every one of them. He had slaughtered the Passover offering and roasted it in the fat, while Sarah, the Messiah's wife, sat in the Sultan's chair, where she was served by caliphs and pashas. Scholars and holy men had kissed her feet and heard the mysteries of the Torah from her lips. Wearing the crown of King David, Sabbatai Zevi had been surrounded by the Fathers, who had risen from their sepulchers in the Cave of Machpaleh. Every day Sabbatai Zevi journeyed to the seashore to re-

ceive the potentates who arrived in sailing vessels
from the other side of the River Samation, bringing
with them talents of gold and precious stones sent
by the king of the Ten Tribes. Fifty knights rode
before the Messiah, singers attended him with songs
of praise, glorifying the Almighty. The earth was
cleft by the sound of their voices. . . .

The opponents of Sabbatai Zevi were silenced.
Some of them now believed in him; others out of
fear of persecution said nothing. In the study house
the young men pored over the account of the building of the Holy Temple, and those descended from
priests studied the offerings and the sprinkling of
sacrificial blood on the altar. As soon as night fell,
fiery omens appeared in the sky. One night Rechele,
looking into her broth, saw seven maidens with
golden crowns on their heads and heard the sweet
strains of an unearthly melody. Revealing her secret
to no one, she immediately set out to tell Reb
Gedaliya.

Reb Gedaliya happened to be all alone in the
house. A wax candle burned in a silver candlestick;
on the table stood an earthen jug of wine; on a silver
platter lay a roast hen. Before Rechele could speak,
Reb Gedaliya rose and ran to meet her with outstretched arms, crying:

"Welcome, O righteous woman, in God's name!
Verily, I know all!" And he shut the door behind her.

❦ 5 ❦

Rechele Prophesies

Midnight of the fourteenth day of the month of
Sivan, in early June, Rechele lying in her canopy
bed after a penitential fast (Reb Itche Mates had
lodged in the study house overnight), heard a sound
as of the wind blowing and wings beating. A bright
red glow surrounded her; flames seemed to over-
whelm the house, and a voice called:

"Rechele, Rechele!"

"Speak, for thy servant hearkeneth," replied
Rechele, who had studied the Bible and remembered
the tale of the young Samuel and Eli, the priest.

"Rechele, be strong and of good cheer! I am the Angel Sandalfon!" an awesome voice said. "For lo, I shall put thy tears into a gourd and bear them up on high to the Throne of Glory. Thy prayers and supplications have penetrated the seven firmaments. Go, and proclaim in the ears of those that tremble at the word of God that the perfect and full redemption will come at the new year. And to Reb Gedaliya, that saintly man, thou shalt announce: 'All the worlds on high do tremble at the unions he doth form. The power of his combinations reaches even to the heavenly mansions. From these combinations seraphim and angels twist coronets for the Divine Presence.' "

All night the voice called to Rechele, without interruption, at times in the holy tongue, at times in Yiddish. The air thickened with smoke and a glowing, ghostly, purple light. Rechele felt the walls sundering, the ceiling dissolving, and the whole house above the clouds. Swooning with fear, she lay with inert limbs: her eyes glazed, her arms and legs distended and wooden like those of a corpse. With the rising of the morning star, at cockcrow, the voice subsided, but Rechele did not stir until sunrise. Only then did she waken and rouse from her swoon. Her ears still rang with the voice, her cheeks were damp with tears, and her body strange and cold, like one returned from the edge of death. Yet she rose from her bed on faltering legs, washed at the full tun, rinsing her breasts and thighs as though performing a ritual.

Then, dressing in her Sabbath garments, she put on her jewelry, covered her face with a veil, and set out for the prayer-house court. Those who passed her were astonished to see her dressed so. Some thought her in the power of an evil spirit. Others followed her to see what would happen, for they surmised at once that this was no ordinary occasion. No sooner had Rechele crossed the study house threshold than she fell face forward on the earth. Though in the midst of prayer, the worshipers saw Rechele fall, and the Eighteen Benedictions were interrupted. Reb Gedaliya, who was putting away his phylacteries in their silver container, dropped them in consternation. Some men approached the woman, intending to assist her, for they thought this some human affliction. But suddenly a voice issued from Rechele; it resounded from wall to wall:

"O Jews! Happy are you, and happy your souls! I have beheld a great light. At midnight the great and awful Angel Sandalfon came to me. He announced wondrous things. At the time of the new year good shall come to us, for the godfearing shall gather in Jerusalem. Be strong and of good cheer, O Jews, and proclaim a fast. And as for the saintly man, Reb Gedaliya, the Angel declared: 'The time has come for him to be revealed. For he is a godly man, and worthy, like Elijah, to behold the face of the Divine Presence.' "

Rechele spoke in fits and starts, as though in her sleep, but so resonant was her voice that its echo could be heard throughout the town, and the people of Goray came running. Shopkeepers deserted their shops, artisans rushed in with sack aprons circling their loins, women left sucklings in their cradles, and flew breathless into the study house. Young men and girls leaped up on tables, hung onto bookshelves, climbed the very walls to see what was happening. Pranksters climbed into the study house through the window, and someone accidentally knocked against the copper candelabrum, and there was a shouting and a furor, for it was in danger of falling and causing disaster. Hearing the news, an old paralyzed woman who sat at her spinning wheel pulled on her dress and ran to look at the prophetess. But so great was the confusion that no one noticed this marvel. Meanwhile, Rechele, with arms and legs extended, still lay there, baring mysteries of mysteries, such as no son of man had ever heard—much less a woman. Calling by name angels and seraphim, she told of the heavenly mansions and the lords ruling in each of them; the cryptic passages in the Book of Daniel so baffling to ordinary minds were explained by her— it was clear to all that the spirit of prophecy had entered into Rechele. Several individuals fainted. A shudder ran through the crowd, for no one in Goray had ever witnessed anything like this, and it was interpreted as a sign that God had taken compassion on his congregation and the end of days was near.

Reb Gedaliya bent over Rechele, listening to the voice and trembling with fear; his body had to be supported by two strong men, for his legs had failed him, and he shook as with fever. Only when Rechele lay as though dead, did Reb Gedaliya gesture for a prayer shawl to cover her face. Then he bore her in his arms to the dais.

So tightly was the study hall packed, there was not even room for a pin. However, the crowd made way for Rechele, as though she were the sacred Torah. Some even touched her with their fingertips as she passed and bore their fingers to their lips, as when a scroll is taken from the Ark. Rechele's left shoe fell and Reb Godel lifted it like some holy vessel. Reb Gedaliya placed Rechele on the dais table and commanded that candles be lighted in the menorah. Then he approached the woman, kissed her forehead, and said in a wavering voice, for his throat was full of tears:

"Rechele, my daughter, be of stout heart! Happy are we, for the Divine Presence has returned to us, and happy art thou, for she has chosen thee!"

The study house was filled with the sounds of sobbing women and whispering men. Anxiously all waited for the prophetess to begin again. Rechele opened her eyes.

Her sick body shivered, as with cold, and her teeth chattered. She seemed to struggle with a compulsion to speak, but her strength deserted her again, and she uttered a shrill wail. Then, sighing, she grew still once more, as though her soul had deserted her. Reb Gedaliya straightened up and lifted his arms,

signaling silence. His silk coat flew open, the crown
of his hat pointed skyward, and his whole figure was
imbued with the awe of Heaven. He resembled one
of those great men of old, a leader of Israel.

"Jews!" he cried. "The blessed God has worked a
great miracle for us! The Angel Sandalfon has
spoken to us this day through the lips of Rechele!
Prophecy has returned! Let us all recite the benediction of thanks!"

"Blessed art thou, O Lord, our God, king of the
universe, who hath kept us alive, and sustained us,
and brought us to this day!" every mouth responded.
The walls shook with the echo, and the very pillars
of the dais seemed to rock.

"Let us send forth emissaries! Let us spread the
word to every settlement!"

"I'll go!" shouted someone; it was lame Mordecai
Joseph. "I'll run and waken the whole world!"

"Go, Mordecai Joseph!" Reb Gedaliya cried, "and
take with you Itche Mates, the husband of the prophetess! Do not hesitate—spread the news!"

"Where is Itche Mates?"

"Bring Itche Mates!" rasped Reb Mordecai
Joseph, and he held his head with his hands, as
though he were going mad. He threw his crutch from
him.

All his life Reb Mordecai Joseph, the cabalist and
student of mysteries, had anticipated the day when
his mission would be to go into the world. He had
always feared that his revelations and warnings

would find no listeners, for his name was unknown outside of Goray. But now Reb Mordecai Joseph's voice could resound throughout all Poland, stirring up every community. He already imagined himself in Lublin at the yearly fair, standing before the assembly of the Council of the Four Lands, roaring with his lion's voice at multitudes of important Jews —rabbis, righteous men, learned men, rich men— pouring pitch and tar on those who doubted Sabbatai Zevi, bidding that they be flogged and bound with heavy ropes. Their tracts and epistles must be burned in a fire whose glow would reach Heaven. In his enthusiasm Reb Mordecai Joseph began to preach standing there in the study house at Goray.

"I swear by the Messiah of the God of Jacob that Rechele is a true prophetess! Woe to the doubters! Alas for their souls! A curse on them! May they perish! Do you hear me, men? May they be torn out by the roots! But O you true believers, rejoice in the Lord!"

Reb Mordecai Joseph suffered a coughing spasm and then suddenly Reb Gedaliya lifted Rechele in his arms and walked in the direction of the doorway to the anteroom. Song burst from every throat. Men and women embraced, kissed, and, with arms about each other, danced out of the study house. Hats and bonnets fell from their heads, but no one cared. The gentiles who had crowded about the prayer house stepped back, terrified at the sight; they kneeled and bowed, and God's name was sanctified abroad. Young

men took the Torah scrolls, and the curtain of the
Ark was hung on poles as a kind of canopy and borne
aloft over the heads of Reb Gedaliya and Rechele.
Never since Goray first became a town had there been
such rejoicing. Even the ill and bedridden were taken
from the poorhouse to witness the holiday. A few
apprentices in their zeal fetched the board of purification and burned it in the midst of the market
place, as a sign that death from this day on should
cease among Jews. And that very day, Reb Mordecai
Joseph and Reb Itche Mates, taking parchment letters written by Reb Gedaliya and Levi and signed
by many witnesses, hung beggars' bags on their arms
and went off to spread the news far and wide—that
they might gladden the hearts of those who believed
in God and in Sabbatai Zevi, His Messiah.

❦ 6 ❦

A Wedding on a Dung-Hill

Reb Mordecai Joseph and Reb Itche Mates departed, and their wanderings took them to far places, bearing the good tidings. In Goray some believed that they had already passed the Polish borders and were now somewhere in Germany, or Bohemia. Others thought that the emissaries had embarked for Stamboul to see the Messiah. Now the affairs of Goray town were managed by Reb Gedaliya. His new rulings disagreed with the practices cited in the Shulchan Aruch, but the few learned men who remained pretended neither to see nor hear what was happening, for the common people believed in Reb Gedaliya. As for Reb Gedaliya, he settled Rechele in his house, and he lived with her under one roof although she was a matron. He had a room painted white for her, and he hung the walls with guardian amulets, and placed a Holy Ark and Torah there. Rechele was dressed in white satin; her face was hidden by a veil. During the week she could be seen by no one except Chinkele the Pious who served her. But on the Sabbath ten women from the sect gathered in her room to make a prayer quorum, as though they were men— for thus Reb Gedaliya had bidden. A woman cantor stood before the lectern chanting the Sabbath prayers. Then the scroll was taken from the Ark and Reb Gedaliya chanted the proper melody. Moreover, he permitted seven women to be called up to the lectern to read for the Sabbath, and after each reading he ordered a benediction of thanks to be offered in the name of Sabbatai Zevi and Rechele the prophetess.

His was a great name in Goray and in all of the surrounding countryside. Housewives gave him a tithe of their chickens, eggs, butter, and honey. A special poll tax had been laid by him on the rich. From every calf he slaughtered he put aside for himself not only the tripe and the milt, as the custom is, but all of the under-parts as well—these he cleaned, though it is not the practice to do so nowadays. He did not need these for himself, no, not Reb Gedaliya —but for the poor and hungry. Sabbath afternoons he held the midday feast in the study house, and every household sent him pudding, seasoned according to his taste. Men and women sat at the table on benches, or clustered about it, and Reb Gedaliya sang new Sabbath hymns, served portions of calf's foot jelly himself, and gave each person a cup of wine. The wine was red and smelled of ginger, onycha, and saffron. Reb Gedaliya hinted that it tasted like the wine reserved for the righteous to drink in the Garden of Eden.

Remarkable things were done by Reb Gedaliya, and his kindness was renowned. He was extremely charitable and would rise from bed in the middle of night to tend to the sick. Though an important man, he would roll up his sleeves when it was necessary, to massage men and women alike with aqua vitae and turpentine. He jested with the ill, forcing them to laugh and forget their pains. For children he imitated the mooing of cows and the twittering of birds. Stammerers began to speak properly under his guidance. The melancholy laughed heartily after he had spent some time with them. Adept at sleight of hand and hocus-pocus, he could turn a kerchief into a hare. His elbows bound with a sash, he would blow, freeing them once more—and then produce the sash from beneath the shirt of the person who had bound him! An expert at solving complex puzzles, he could write a row of words that might be read from top to bottom as well as the usual Hebrew right to left. He showed housewives who came to visit him how to put up new kinds of preserves, taught girls how to work on canvas and embroider. In the late afternoon he bathed in the river and instructed the young men how to swim and tread water. Afterward they all said their afternoon prayers at the riverbank, under the open sky. Once, when in good spirits, he gathered a few lusty young fellows who were boarding at their in-laws and went to the other side of the hill to scare the women bathing there. Chaos ensued. The more agile women sprang screaming into the water. Those who were large and slow-moving were so confused that they remained transfixed. Uncovered before the eyes of the men, they were publicly shamed. There was much jesting and frivolity that evening. Nevertheless, this was not taken amiss in Reb Gedaliya, for he was already known for his unconventional ways. Only a few hidden foes spoke out against him, with no attempt to disguise their irritation.

They whispered unpleasant things about him. They said that since becoming the slaughterer of Goray he had never once found any beast to be unclean and unfit to be eaten—this in order to win the favor of the butchers. Whenever the question arose, he ruled the beast clean, and he had abandoned all the laws of purity. He permitted the women to go to the bathhouse and then to bed with their husbands soon after menstruation; according to him, they did not have to keep the additional seven days of abstinence. He explained to young matrons ways to enflame their husbands, and whispered in their ears that, ever since Sabbatai Zevi had been revealed, the commandment against adultery was void. It was rumored that young men were exchanging wives, and everyone knew that Nechele, the wife of Levi, received men in her house and sat up past midnight with them, singing prurient songs. A servant girl who had been sent to look through the keyhole was said to have seen Nechele unhooking her blouse and offering the visitors her breasts to press and the nipples to be kissed. Of Levi it was said that he had forced Glicke, his brother Ozer's daughter, to lie with him, and that he had paid Ozer three Polish gold coins as requital money, that the sin might not be discovered. The young men who studied together in the study house were up to all kinds of evil. They would climb into the women's gallery in the middle of the day, committing pederasty with one another, and sodomy —with the goats. Evenings they went to the bathhouse and, through a hole they had bored in the wall, watched the women purifying themselves. Other young scholars even went off to observe the women tending to their bodily needs. . . .

There were few old householders in Goray, and no one heeded their grumbling. Reb Gedaliya bribed some with rich gifts. Others were warned that, if they rebelled against his rule, he would place them under a ban, or have them arrested and bound to the post in the study house anteroom. He also presented himself before the lord of Goray; speaking a fluent Polish, he gained the lord's promise to take him under his protection and punish those who tried to overthrow him.

Goray, that small town at the edge of the world, was altered. No one recognized it any longer.

Ever since the advent of Reb Gedaliya and since the miracle of the prophetess, the town had prospered. From Yanov, Bilgoray, Krasnistav, Turbin, Tishevitz, and other settlements, people came to visit the holy pair. The water in which Rechele washed her body had restoring powers, Reb Gedaliya proclaimed, and a barrel of it stood in the anteroom of his house. The dispirited who wandered from place to place in search of a cure came to Goray. They gathered before the porch of Reb Gedaliya's house: young women whose hiccuping was like the barking of dogs; barren women who yearned for a blessing that might unlock their wombs; monstrosities, with reptile outlines on their bodies; paralytics and epileptics. Chinkele the Pious stood at the door and let them in one by one. Many of the visitors had to wait at the Goray inns for a long time before being admitted to Reb Gedaliya's house, so they might receive from him amulets and pieces of magical amber and salves to be smeared on the disturbed part of the body and pills to be swallowed. He licked the faces of sickly children, massaged arthritic women, and had them spend the night in his house. Daily the number who came to the miracle worker increased. They shopped in Goray, and slept on the bare floor in the

homes of the townsfolk, avidly listening to the amazing tales concerning Rechele the prophetess. Everywhere, they sat on benches in front of the houses.
Their kerchiefs were pulled down over their eyes;
their hands clutched baskets of food; between their
breasts hung pouches containing the copper coins
that were to buy them health. The young were bashful, and would say nothing. But the older women
knitted stockings and recounted with relish their sick-
nesses and the cures they had been given by various
magicians and miracle workers. Those whose men-
strual flow had stopped prematurely were advised to
eat the foreskin of a circumcised infant. Those who
wished to please their husbands were told to have
their men drink the water in which their breasts had
been washed; those with the falling sickness were
told to cut the nails of their hands and feet and have
the nails kneaded into a lump of dough and thrown
to a dog. At times older women would tease the
young barren ones, shocking them with their lewd
talk.

And then, finally, men also began to arrive in the
town. There were beggars and vagabonds; there were
ascetics, and there were husbands trying to get the
signatures of a hundred rabbis for a writ of remar-
riage; a yeshiva student was seeking a master to teach
him cabala; a penitent was tormenting himself by
putting peas in his shoes. A convert from Amsterdam
also came, a man who had taken a vow of silence as
well as a bandsman who walked around blindfolded,

so as not to perceive women, and a barefoot jester who asked for alms and recited obscene rhymes. These lived by begging from the pilgrims, slept in the poorhouse or, when that was full, in any corner they could find. Evil often transpired secretly. Once two wandering beggars who had come to Goray decided to marry, and married they were by some mischief makers on a dung-hill.

❧ 7 ❧

The Hour of Union

This was a year of severe drought. The grass that was to be used as fodder had been scorched, and the peasants sold their beasts at half-price. Wheat grew sparsely in the fields, and the stalks were light and empty. Burning winds threshed the yet unreaped grain, and ripped the green fruit from the trees. Every day a host of peasants passed through Goray on their way to chapels and shrines to pray for rain. They were so poor that the men wore straw for clothing. Their cheeks were hollow, and their protruding, frightened eyes stared from beneath their strands of flaxen hair like the eyes of madmen. The women carried their babies on their backs, wrapped in sheets, gypsy fashion. The feet of these wanderers were black from the dust of the roads, their voices were hoarse from imploring their God, and it seemed as if they had already died, and that this entourage was conducting itself to the grave. The rumor in the villages was that, before going off to join their Messiah, the Jews had prevailed upon the devil to kill all Christians. Each day the water sprite carried off another Christian; the water sprite was large as a cow, and swam backward in the river which he patroled early each evening in search of victims; his custom was to sing and do antics to attract the passers-by. Nor was this the only evil the devil concocted. He had of late sent a black cloud of locusts swooping down upon the fields; he had also summoned the field mice of the world and had sent them scampering through the furrows of wheat and into the barns. And one night a peasant saw a spirit dancing on stilts near the windmill. It whirled and capered and whistled, its face bearded, its feet webbed like the feet of a goose. Wild creatures circled it, foxes, and polecats, martens and wolves. They beat their wings like birds, and flew away laughing. A young woman who had gone to the well late one evening to fetch water, felt her bucket touch some live thing, and heard a voice from the depth cry out:

"Sell me thy soul, handsome one. I shall give thee sweet almonds and a string of beads. I shall set a crown on thy head, and thou shalt be my princess."

The peasants in the villages did not speak their wrath. In silence each day they sharpened their scythes, though there was no crop to harvest, in silence they filed the blades of their axes. It was thought by some that they would rise in revolt, murdering the Jews as well as the Polish gentry. Others predicted Cossack armies advancing from the Ukraine and Wolhynia, as in Chmelnicki's days, to avenge the oppression of the people. As if this were not enough, there was an increase in the number of practitioners of the evil eye. Cattle stopped giving milk and women turned yellow with jaundice. In the village of Kotzitza the householders buried a witch alive. They nailed a horseshoe to her left foot to prevent her from running from her grave, and they stuffed her mouth with poppy seed. In the village of Maidan the peasants lured a witch into the woods, chained her to a tree, and built a fire about her, after stripping her of her clothes. The villagers watched the naked witch writhe and tear at her flesh in agony, calling upon the name of Satan, until the flames consumed her. Then four women hacked her body to pieces with sickles, and buried the corpse in a field, with neither mound nor cross to show where she lay.

The most ancient in Goray could not remember such a time. It was difficult to get a loaf of bread, but meat was plentiful. Early each evening the butcher boys drove whole herds of calves, and sheep, and goats to the slaughterhouse. They brought cows whose udders had shrunken and had ceased giving milk. These animals had thin flanks overgrown with thick clumps of dung; their ribs stuck out like barrel staves; their bellies hung loose like empty bags; their black, damp, hairy muzzles were drawn with hunger and thirst; and the town resounded with their pitiful mooing. They fell at the butcher's first push, and expired without a struggle. Reb Gedaliya hurried about with his green slaughtering knife, expertly slashing at the shaven necks, and recoiling from the spatter of blood. Butchers moved about with hatchets chopping off the heads of the still breathing beasts, dexterously stripping hides, tearing bodies open, and dragging out red satin lungs, half-empty stomachs, and intestines. They inflated the lungs by blowing through the windpipe, and slapped the distended organs and spat into the flaps to see if there were any vents which would make the animal unclean. Reb Gedaliya stood in the center of the slaughterhouse, his knife clenched between his teeth, his earlocks and his long beard disheveled, his black eyes, deep set in the hairy pouches of his cheeks, rolling as he urged the butchers to finish the examination, remonstrating:

"Hurry! It's clean! It's clean!"

For Reb Gedaliya had to be very sparing of his time; the weight of all Goray lay on his shoulders. The elders waited at the town meeting to hear his views; the women required his advice on how to obtain dowries for orphan girls; it was he whom the lord of Goray had licensed to levy and collect taxes, in his wisdom; emissaries brought him letters from the Sabbatai Zevi sect in Zamosc and Ludomir; rich men from other towns pleaded for his salves and potions; persons possessed, brides under a spell, children with blown-up bellies were brought to him. The table in Reb Gedaliya's room was piled high with sheaves of parchment, goose-quill pens, hailstones from Heaven, balls of devil-dung. There was always a pot of leeches handy, and somewhere in the room Reb Gedaliya had a scroll inscribed with the names of angels and demons. Secreted elsewhere was a black-bordered mirror and a cross on a string of beads. Young men frequently came to study the circulars of Nathan of Gaza and Abraham Ha-Yachini. Reb Gedaliya trained these young men in the magical science of drawing wine from walls, and transporting themselves from place to place according to a cabalistic formula. . . .

Goray was elated. Every few days there was another wedding. Twelve-year-old brides walked the streets with swollen bellies, for pious women saw to it that their daughters and sons-in-law lay with each other often. Moreover, Reb Gedaliya and Levi had released from marriage all women who had been deserted—and they had lost no time finding new husbands. Reb Gedaliya's calculations were that the ram's horn would announce the coming of the Messiah in the middle of the month of Elul, and three days before Rosh Hashana a cloud would descend and the pious would climb aboard and be off to the Land of Israel. Daily, between the afternoon and the evening prayers, Reb Gedaliya told the congregation of the miracles that were about to take place. Every godfearing man would have ten thousand heathen slaves to wash his feet and care for him. Duchesses and princesses would act as the nurses and governesses of Jewish children, as had been foretold in the Book of Isaiah; thrice daily the Jews would fly like eagles to the mount of the Lord and there bow and prostrate themselves before the Holy Temple. The afflicted would be healed, the ugly made beautiful. Everyone would eat from golden dishes and drink only wine. The daughters of Israel would bathe in streams of balsam, and the fragrance of their bodies would suffuse the world. The sons of Israel would go girded in armor, swords on their thighs and equipped with bows and arrows with which to harry the remnants of the foes of Israel. Those of the nobility who had been kind to the children of Israel would be spared, along with their wives and children; they would be the servants of the upright.

As the month of Elul approached, the faith of the people of Goray grew stronger. Shopkeepers no longer kept shop, artisans suspended their labors. It seemed useless to complete anything. Now the people ate only food that did not need preparation and was easy to obtain. Since they were too slothful to gather firewood in the forest, they acquired the habit of heating their ovens with the lumber they had avail-

able. By winter they would be settled in Jerusalem.
And so they tore down fences and outhouses for kindling. Some even ripped the shingles from their
roofs. Many refused to undress when they retired at
night. The awaited cloud might come when they
were asleep, and they did not wish to be forced to
dress in a hurry. In Reb Godel Chasid's house the
books had been wrapped in a sheet, as after a fire,
and thrice daily their owner stepped outside to look
toward the east for some sign of the cloud. He would
cover his eyes, as though to protect them from too
strong a light, and cry:

"Father in Heaven, save us now. We have not the
strength to wait longer."

Late at night Reb Gedaliya would come to visit
Rechele in her room. She would be lying in her
canopy bed, asleep. Since becoming a prophetess,
Rechele had almost ceased eating entirely; no longer
did she attend to her physical needs. Her body had
become white and semi-transparent, like mother-of-
pearl, and it seemed to her that she was exuding a
leafy fragrance. Each night angels visited her in her
dreams, and Rabbi Simeon ben Yohai and the
prophet Elijah came, and angels and prophets studied
with her until daybreak. Often when she awoke in
the morning she would be able to recite entire sections from the Zohar and its Emendations by heart.
At times she spoke to Reb Gedaliya in Targum
Aramaic. As she read the pages turned of their own
accord. Sometimes she would put out her hand to

take some object, and it would fly to her fingers, as though drawn by magic. Her body shone in the darkness like a precious stone, and her skin emitted sparks. She would lie in her canopy bed wearing a silk kerchief on her head, which rested on three pillows, one of her eyes half open, her nose white, her breathing so faint it could not be heard. Reb Gedaliya would enter naked, a thick growth of hair covering his body like a fur coat, wearing only a skull cap, and with a wax candle in his left hand. He would lift the white silk gown that covered Rechele's body, kiss her feet, and waken her.

"Rechele, it is midnight. The heavens are parting. The Divine Parents are coupling face to face. Rechele, be of good cheer. This is the hour of union."

❦ 8 ❦

Golden Jackets and Marzipan Candy

The month of Elul. Each morning crowds of women descended to the cemetery to bid the dead farewell; the dead would not reach the holy land as soon as the living; when the Messiah came they would pass to the Land of Israel by way of underground caverns. For days the women lay prostrate on the graves, screaming and wailing, begging the forgiveness of the dead for deserting them, explaining that the day of resurrection was near, calling upon them to intercede for their living kin and neighbors in the Hereafter. The wealthy cut wicks the length of the graves of their beloved, to make candles for the study house. The poor could only weep, and the graves were wet with their tears. Even the children were brought, and they played among the tombstones. It seemed as if the living and the dead dwelt together in the cemetery, and the gypsies who had pitched their tents close by marveled at the sight. As for the gentiles, they were delighted, believing that they would inherit all that the Jews abandoned. In the study house the ram's horn was sounded, and Reb Godel Chasid trembled at each blast, for each might be the one that announced the Messiah. Too anxious to remain at home, he paced restlessly outside. For several days a cloud had hovered in the sky to the east of Goray. Evenings, it elongated, taking on the shape of an enormous fish; mornings it was aflame, a burning red, and afternoons it seemed a ship with silver sails, drawing nearer and nearer. Reb Godel and the other members of the sect were certain this was the pillar of cloud mentioned in the holy scriptures; but they spoke of this only among themselves in hushed tones, so that the people might not become excited. The women shook their heads piously, unable to keep their eyes away from that part of the sky; all seemed to feel that at such a moment silence was best.

But the days came and went, and still there was no miracle.

As the High Holy Day grew nearer, Goray grew quieter and quieter. It was as if the inhabitants of the town had deserted it one by one, or had gone into hiding. The curtains of the houses were drawn; here and there shutters were bolted. The shops were either closed or were tended by children. The market was empty; the sand in the market place was hot as in a desert, and nettles grew at the edge of the circle. The whole town seemed to be holding its breath. When people met they discoursed in whispers, and they avoided each other's eyes. In this hour of eclipse they seemed to be dazzled.

Only three days remained before the eve of the High Holy Day, and according to all calculations this was the day on which the great blast was to be heard. But the sun set—and nothing had occurred. Nor had the people of Goray prepared for the holy days. Children and adults went barefoot and in tatters; there was no flour with which to bake the bread for the holy days; there was no fish or honey. Reb Gedaliya was sought to explain the significance of this, but it was discovered that he had gone to commune in the hills. As for Rechele, she had been in a coma for several days, and Chinkele would permit no one to see her. At the last moment runners had been sent out to the surrounding villages to buy the most necessary articles. But they had not as yet returned. The unpainted houses huddled together, their roofs torn and their interiors visible: dusty attics full of cobwebs and rubbish. That summer the people of Goray had destroyed their most valuable possessions: they had ripped up floors and dismembered chests and shelves. At Reb Godel Chasid's they had burned the wall beams in the oven on Friday. All the holiday clothes were soiled and torn because the women had worn them on weekdays.

Never before had there been such weeping as this year at the Penitential Prayers. No sooner had the Prayer of Sanctification begun than the cantor fell to the ground, as though his legs had collapsed beneath him. At the words, "Behold, I will turn the captivity of Jacob's tents," the congregation burst into lamentation. One old man beat his head with his fists, and cried: "Father in Heaven, you have tested us sufficiently! Now display your might!"

Rosh Hashana eve was cool and damp. The sky, which all summer long had been as blue as the curtain of the Torah Ark, and somewhat broader and higher than usual, contracted. Now the town seemed enclosed in a dark canvas tent. The hills, which had been green and evocative of the holy land, disappeared, wiped off the face of the earth. The smoke, reluctant to leave the chimneys, spread over the houses, as though space had shrunken.

Not until sunset did the pious lose hope in the possibility of a miracle. Miracles, they knew, always occur unexpectedly, when people are looking the other way. Perhaps just an instant before sunset the cloud would appear and carry them all off to the holy land. Some had even had a presentiment that it would happen thus. Reb Godel Chasid was steadfast; God, he argued, was testing the people of Goray to see whether they truly believed in Him with their whole heart. He went so far in his obstinacy that it angered him to see his household preparing food; he put out the fire in the oven, so certain that the evening meal would be eaten in the Land of Israel. Not until it grew dark and the stars could be seen peeping through the clouds did it become clear to the people of Goray that the Exile was to continue during the High Holy Days. The women sat with downcast eyes and rigid bodies in the unlit houses. The unkempt men hastened to the prayer house, unwashed and with straggly beards. Too ashamed to commune with one another, they immediately began the long overdue afternoon prayers.

Reb Gedaliya had returned from the hills a few hours before. He stood at the lectern reading the evening prayers, singing in a loud tearful voice and completely enveloped in his prayer shawl and white robe. His every groan set the congregation shaking, like trees in a storm. The women wailed as though they were mourning for the dead. After the prayers, the worshipers left quickly, without wishing one another a happy new year. There were no candles in town, and so the people of Goray sat in the darkness that night, or burned kindling chips. At the holiday feast they had nothing but meat and last year's kidney beans, though they were weary of meat. Those who were fortunate enough to have a loaf of bread divided it into slices which were sent their relatives to share. The children cried hard, complaining that they had been fooled. . . . They wanted to go to

Jerusalem. . . . They wanted to wear little golden
jackets. . . . They wanted wings, so they could fly
through the air. . . . They wanted the marzipan
candy and the gold coins in the broth that they had
been promised. . . . Their fathers looked dejected
and toyed with the food, eating merely to fulfill the
religious duty, in order not to appear to be fasting
on Rosh Hashana. They sang the High Holy Day
hymns with hoarse, quavering voices and quickly
went off to sleep behind the oven, silent and irri-
table. Mothers quieted the sucklings by nursing them,
and sat up late next to the children's cribs and
beds, sleepily telling stories to keep the little ones
from asking questions. Though it was a High Holy
Day, the silent feuds between mother-in-law and
daughter-in-law, mother and daughter, brother and
sister, persisted, as bitter as ever. The people of
Goray fell asleep in their clothes, their mouths open
and their hearts hollow, as in times of persecution
when Jews are never sure that they will live through
the next day.

On both the first and the second day of Rosh
Hashana Reb Gedaliya preached before the ram's
horn was blown. His face was cinder-red, his eyes
flashed, and every word he spoke lightened the heart
of the congregation. He argued that this marred holiday was the last of the trials that God was inflicting
on his people. Reb Gedaliya compared the present
time to the hour before dawn, when the sky must
become darkest so that the sun might shine forth in

all its splendor. He called on all in the congregation
to be steadfast in their faith, and not to despair on
this eve of great days. He swore a mighty oath that
Sabbatai Zevi was the true Messiah of the God of
Jacob; he bade the Jews put away their sadness and
gird themselves with trust and joy; he said that the
Four Matriarchs had visited Rechele at night to solace
her, and they had reported that Satan had leveled a
bitter accusation in Heaven against those who wavered in their faith; as a consequence, the end of
days had been postponed until such time as the wrath
of God should be placated. Before the congregation
dispersed, Reb Gedaliya blessed each worshiper with
his hands. He lifted the children to kiss them on the
head, and called out as the congregation departed:

"Go home and rejoice. We shall all be in the Land
of Israel soon, speedily and in our time. Every man
shall sit under his vine and under his fig tree."

For the ceremony of the Casting, everyone in town
put on his or her holiday rags and, walking in file,
set forth in the direction of the river outside the town.
Rechele, who was not well, was borne on a gilded
chair, and accompanied by the most important
people in town. She looked (impossible comparison!)
like one of those icons that the gentiles bear in
church processions during their festivals. . . . The
young women stood on the bridge and shook out
their pockets and kerchiefs, alluding to the transgressions that are cast into running waters. As was
customary, the younger people of Goray were jolly

at the expense of the old women and even the men.
They jibed at Nechele, Levi's wife, whispering in
one another's ears that the river would overflow with
her sins. Returning to town, uncouth boys tried to
stab the women's hips with pins and made lewd remarks. Reb Godel Chasid shouted angrily, repri-
manding them for being sacrilegious; but Reb
Gedaliya passed it off with a wave of his hand, signifying that there was no harm in raising people's
spirits. . . . Nevertheless, at dusk the town grew so
still one might have thought that everyone had died.
The air turned blue, like the pages of an old book,
the houses were drab, half in ruins, and it seemed
like the year 1648. The pails of water that the girls
carried were reminiscent of ablution rites for the
dead, and everything smelled burned and acrid,
as after a fire. Sleepily, the men recited psalms in the
study house, as though they were asking for com-
passion on some person who was mortally ill. The
women gathered before the doors of their homes.
They spoke in hushed tones, looking around them
meanwhile, fearful of being overheard by strangers;
they let the children pull the last embellishments
from their coats, just so that they—the mothers—
might have some peace. One woman casually remarked that people ought to repair their houses and
get this thing out of their heads; the Messiah was
not coming to Goray. But the other women scolded
her. They threatened her, warning her to be silent.
She was reminded that she was no one, a person of

humble origin. The women shook their heads and spat; they blew their noses piously and entreated the Almighty:

"May it be thy will, O Father in Heaven, that this holy day be the last to be spoiled! May we soon have true cause to rejoice—after such humiliation!"

❦ 9 ❦

The Evil One Triumphs

On the first day of the Feast of Tabernacles a deluge descended on Goray, and the rain poured down incessantly for three days and three nights. The river overflowed, smashing the locks of the water mill and crumbling the dam. Those who dwelt in the lowlands had to be rescued. In many homes women waded about, their dresses lifted, bailing out the water with pots and buckets, only to find it pouring in once more. Icy winds tore the last shingles from the roofs and knocked down fences. The windows were covered with rags and felt was plugged in the cracks.

Very little wood could be obtained. The children began to cough, and developed red noses and watery
eyes. Their ears, which had been healed by the
summer sun, began to run anew; boils that had dried
up swelled up again. Their stomachs ached from
eating too much meat, and there were many cases of
vomiting and diarrhea. Mothers ran to the study
house to implore God's help, and lit candles in every
candle holder. Groups of school boys went to the
study house to recite psalms. Nevertheless, in house
after house infants succumbed, coughing, eventually
to be seized with spasms and turn blue. Joel the Sex-
ton again made the rounds with his black basket.
There were so many children for him to bury that
he had to wrap the infants in linen and stuff them
into the deep pockets of his overcoat. When the
storm subsided, flocks of crows appeared, flying low,
crookedly, and croaking, as though they hunted
corpses. The swamp was oily yellow, and spirals of
vapor rose from it, as from a subterranean fire. It
suggested Sodom and Gomorrah, where the smoke
rose as from a furnace. . . .

The oldest people in Goray could not remember
another Feast of Tabernacles like this, nor had they
ever heard of anything like it from *their* elders. On
the morning of the third day of the holiday week it
suddenly grew dark as night, and everyone at once began to prepare for the worst, for the world seemed to
be about to come to an end. The day before Hoshana
Rabba there was a hailstorm. Pieces of ice fell, large

as goose eggs, injuring many beasts in the meadow, as well as shepherds. Afterward, it began to thunder and lightning, though that was unusual for this time of year. A blinding spiral of fire twisted into the study house, rolled across the tables, like a ball, swirled into the open oven door, and went out the chimney with so loud a crash that many people were deafened. From the study house the lightning flew off to the church, causing considerable damage. On the night of Hoshana Rabba a dreadful thing happened: A woman who had gone to fetch water was thrown by demons into the well, where she was found dead the next morning, head down and feet up. The evil spirits also molested the old night watchman, tearing off half his beard.

During prayers in the study house on Shemini Atzeret a completely unexpected fight broke out which was without precedent in Goray. Later, no one could tell exactly how it started. Some people stated that one of Reb Gedaliya's enemies had struck him in the face. Others insisted that "the others" had had a hand in the affair, for a strange man was said to have appeared among the congregation, only to slink out of sight later. Whatever the cause, there were sudden shouts and cries of pain, as during a bandit attack, and a wild bloody fight ensued. The Sabbatai Zevi sect hurled themselves murderously at their opponents, whom they beat and trampled underfoot, ruining their clothes and prayer shawls. Even the women, as though devil-driven, attacked one another remorselessly, tearing bonnets, ripping shawls and jackets, savagely digging their nails into flesh, and filling the prayer house with their uproar. It took Reb Gedaliya and a few other sensible persons a long time and a great deal of effort to separate and calm the factions, for even the old people had become involved in the battle. Reb Godel Chasid's entire body was one big bruise. In the turmoil, even children and invalids were injured. And, as though this event were not outrageous enough, the next morning, at the Feast of the Rejoicing of the Torah, a band of idlers gathered together and to begin with took over the tavern, like bandits, consuming a whole barrel of aqua vitae. Then they went from house to house singing and snatching up geese, pots full of fat and preserves, and anything drinkable that they found. Nor did they spare Reb Gedaliya. They hastened to his house also, but he was too cunning for them. He came out to meet them, and opening his closets and pantries bade them take whatever their hearts desired, for it was proper to rejoice on such a day. Thus he won favor in their eyes and they showed him respect, calling him "Rabbi." Then they departed drunkenly to the back streets where the common people lived and desecrated the holiday in other ways.

From that time on, not a day passed without incident or affliction. In the middle of the night, at the end of the month of Cheshvan, the earth was heard to rumble and the houses quaked. Everyone ran terrified into the street, unclothed; although the noise stopped, they remained outdoors for hours, afraid to return to their homes. Several developed colds from this and inflammation of the lungs. A few days later a fault was discovered in the prayer-house wall, extending from the roof to the foundation, and it was rumored to be unsafe to worship there, since the walls might collapse; this produced a new furor in the town.

On the fifteenth day of the month of Kislev, in the midst of the morning prayer, the door of the study house suddenly opened, revealing two unexpected visitors: the emissaries, Reb Mordecai Joseph and Reb Itche Mates. Their abject appearance caused universal distress. Reb Mordecai Joseph's feet were bound with rags, his loins covered with a sack, and one of his coat lapels was rent, as though he were in mourning. Reb Itche Mates was barefoot, his body smeared from head to foot with dirt, and his face pot black. The people of Goray were completely taken aback. They were too shocked to open their mouths; they seemed to have lost the power of speech. Finally, some of the worshipers greeted the newcomers; but Reb Mordecai Joseph and Reb Itche Mates did not respond, remaining silent until the whole congregation had gathered around them. Only then did Reb Mordecai Joseph pound his crutch on the floor and beat his breast with his left fist, screaming: "O Jews, rend your garments! Sprinkle ashes on your heads! A great disaster hath overtaken us! A bitter calamity!"

He fell against the wall, gasping until the foam began to ooze out of his mouth; everyone recoiled from him. Then Reb Mordecai Joseph rose to his full height and began again: "He has become a Turk! An apostate! Woe to us that have lived to see this thing! Alas for our souls!"

"Who do you mean, Reb Mordecai Joseph?" many voices implored him, with an anxious presentiment.

"That foul liar!" Reb Mordecai screamed. "That seducer and inciter, Sabbatai Zevi, and his whore Sarah! May they be blotted out! May they be flung from the hollow of the sling! May every curse in the chapter of curses fall on their heads and every plague that afflicted the land of Egypt plague their bodies!"

Reb Itche Mates seated himself on the floor and hid his face. His kaftan was full of holes and his swollen feet were covered with clay. Large yellow tears dripped down his beard, and he swayed to and fro, as though keening over a corpse. Reb Mordecai Joseph's eyes were inflamed, his thick eyebrows prickly, his fiery beard bristled, and he resembled one of the wrathful lions carved in the woodwork above the Holy Ark. He coughed and spat at great length, beating the air with his hairy hands, and sobbing spasmodically, as at a funeral oration.

"He has put on the fez, the mad dog! He worships idols! A great multitude was converted with him! Woe to the unclean! Shame and disgrace for us all!"

All of the congregation bowed their shoulders, as under a heavy burden. They looked exactly as they had that day in the year 1648 when messengers brought them the evil news that Cossacks and Tartars encircled Goray. A young man who fainted easily turned chalk-white, and his neighbors had to hold him by the arms to keep him from slipping to the ground. Even the children froze in their places. Powerless to move, they all stood where they were on quaking feet and with open mouths. Then suddenly the door was violently opened, and Reb Gedaliya rushed into the study house. He had apparently heard all, for on the very threshold he cried with wrathful mockery:

"What is wrong with you, Reb Mordecai Joseph? Why do you cry like a woman in labor?"

"Are *you* still alive!" and Reb Mordecai Joseph sprang to face him. "Devil!"

"Bind him! He is mad!"

"O, thou that sinnest against the God of Israel! Thou adulterer!" Reb Mordecai Joseph roared. "Sabbatai Pig kneels before idols—and this man lies with a married woman!"

"Jews, he is blaspheming!" Reb Gedaliya leaped at Reb Mordecai Joseph and there was the sound of a slap. "He is cursing the Messiah of the Lord of Hosts!"

Reb Mordecai Joseph plunged forward, but he was seized and pulled back. Blood began to flow from his hairy, red nose.

"Woe!" he wailed. "Adultery and bloodshed!"

"Jews, he's lying!" Reb Gedaliya turned to the congregation. "This dog barks lies and deceit. Not Sabbatai Zevi, but Sabbatai Zevi's shadow was converted. There is an explicit passage in the Zohar! The Messiah has ascended to Heaven! He will soon descend and redeem us. Here are letters to prove it! From all the holy men!"

And he drew from his bosom a package of letters and circulars.

Reb Mordecai broke free from the hands of those who were restraining him, threw his crutch into the air, and rushed at Reb Gedaliya with arms outstretched like a beast of prey. But then he fell to earth and lay there hugging the ground and weeping.

"Jews, help! The Evil One triumphs! Woe . . . !"

❦ 10 ❦

The Faithful and Their Opponents

Jews everywhere divided into two factions: that of
Sabbatai Zevi, and their opponents. Controversy
flamed; at every fair the two sects excommunicated
each other with the threefold ritual of ram's horn
blast, purification board, and black candles. Rabbis
were driven from their communities in their stockinged feet, or made to ride in ox-drawn wagons; men
of dignity were flogged publicly and humiliated.
Numerous legates journeyed about, carrying letters,
both authentic and spurious. Traveling prophets and
preachers delivered individual versions of the gospel.

Zealots on both sides were guilty of injustices. In Lublin there were fights in the prayer houses, and Polish soldiers had to separate the participants. In Ludomir the slaughterers thrashed a schoolteacher who forbade people to eat on the Tenth of Tebet. In Hrubishev, only a few persons continued to believe in Sabbatai Zevi, and they were avoided, like lepers, their doors painted with pitch, to signify that none was to cross their thresholds. Moreover, the townspeople banned the sale of food to the Faithful, until they should return to the true faith. The few believers who did repent were treated harshly—they were required to dress in tatters, to cover their heads with ashes, and, lying on the floor of the prayer house anteroom, to pound their breasts while loudly confessing their sins. Everyone who entered or left the study house had to step over them. Some of the worshipers spat in their faces as well.

Certain men of stature in Poland attempted to play the role of peacemaker, but they too became entangled in controversy soon enough and concluded by inciting it even further. The great among the Jews dreaded a widespread desertion of the Jewish faith, as in the days of Anan and the Karaites. It was reported that whole families were being baptized, in every Jewish settlement. Some of the Faithful in such great communities as Jerusalem, Altona, and Vilna committed suicide.

The Faithful themselves were divided into two groups.

One group asserted that the Messiah would not appear until the generation had become completely virtuous. Those persons fasted in penitence, and shunned intercourse with their wives. They mentioned the name of Sabbatai Zevi no less than one hundred times each day, and incised the letters S and Z on their *mezuzot* and windows, on the headboards of their beds, and even on their flesh. They were convinced that Sabbatai Zevi, though a living man, had passed into the World of Emanation, and that the apostate who resided in Stamboul and had taken an Ishmaelitish wife was the demon Ashmodai.

The other group argued that before the Messiah could be revealed he had to enter the Nether Sphere, in order to draw from it the sparks of holiness; there was an explicit text to this effect in the appendix to the Zohar—to wit: *Tov Milgav Ubish* (outwardly evil, inwardly virtuous). Furthermore, the prophet Isaiah had foretold this: "And he shall be reckoned with the sinners." According to those who supported this interpretation, the generation before redemption had to become completely guilty; consequently, they went to great lengths to commit every possible offense. They were secretly adulterous, ate the flesh of the pig and other unclean foods, and performed those labors expressly forbidden on the Sabbath as most to be avoided. In Szebreszin, one such believer shaved off his beard and earlocks with a razor. In the middle of the night, another broke into the prayer house of

Krasnik and corrupted the Torah scrolls by scratching out the name of God. Scribes laid filth in the phylactery boxes that contained verses from the Bible. Other believers defiled the bathhouses, so that the women could not clean themselves properly, and their husbands had to lie with them in their unclean state. Still others threw limbs of corpses into the homes of those of priestly descent, who, as a result, were contaminated. Others went from house to house stealthily putting lard in the pots, thus polluting the food cooked in them. The slaughterer of Kreshev, in order to render slaughtered beasts unkosher, kept his knife unmended; moreover, when he circumcized the new-born, he actually prevented circumcision by not removing the membrane of the corona. The night these things were discovered, the townspeople vengefully surrounded the slaughterer's house. But he slipped away, and his end was unknown. Others of the Faithful spread dissension and calumny. They bore tales to husbands about their wives, and to wives about their husbands; thus frequently incurring violence.

They compelled the pious to desecrate the Sabbath by putting out fires started on Friday night. Divorce often resulted from their rumors of adultery concerning married women. They did not disdain emptying the charity boxes and buying wine to sacrifice to their idols. Their impulse toward corruption led them even to black magic and the conjuring up of the dead.

Though remote from the world, impoverished and bare, Goray found that the dispute did not cease with the conversion of Sabbatai Zevi, but rather increased daily.

Reb Mordecai Joseph, Reb Godel Chasid, and many others abandoned the Faithful and did penance for having succumbed to the seduction of the false redeemer. Reb Godel Chasid dressed in rags and had himself flogged every afternoon, in order to be cleansed of his sin through suffering. Fasting all day until nightfall, he then ate only a bit of bread and garlic. Reb Mordecai Joseph went from house to house agitating against the Faithful. Describing the desolation that followed them everywhere, he gave a long account of their misdeeds, and warned the householders against joining them. Rechele was the only one of the Faithful whom Reb Mordecai Joseph would not vilify. Reb Itche Mates sat locked in an upper-floor room of his father-in-law's house, inscribing his scrolls. He did not pray with the prayer quorum and seldom came outside. No one knew how he subsisted, for he would accept no gift; it was rumored that doves he produced by incantations from the Book of Creation were his food.

Reb Gedaliya and Levi were still leaders of the town. They excommunicated Reb Mordecai Joseph and his supporters, ordering everyone to remain at a distance of four ells from them. Reb Gedaliya and Levi removed many books from the study house and either burned or buried them; all that remained

were volumes of cabalistic mystery. Then they stirred
up hoodlums to ambush Reb Mordecai Joseph behind the bathhouse when he came out to relieve himself. They fell upon him, trampled him with their
feet, rolled him in the dung, and beat him mercilessly
until they thought him dead. Not until many hours
later did the bathhouse attendant find Reb Mordecai
Joseph, his clothing blood-soaked, and both his eyes
blackened. A few days later these very same men compelled Reb Itche Mates to consent to divorce his wife
Rechele—nor did they mind that the river of Goray
had two names, and that the tradition was that no
bill of divorcement could be written in the town.
As for Reb Gedaliya, he did not wait the legal ninety
days; the very next morning he stood with Rechele
under the wedding canopy, thus openly demonstrat-
ing his contempt for the Talmud.

From that time on, Goray indulged in every kind
of license, becoming more corrupt each day. Assured
that every transgression was a rung in the ladder of
self-purification and spiritual elevation, the people
of Goray sank to the forty-nine Gates of Impurity.
Only a few individuals did not join in but stood
apart watching Satan dance in the streets.

And the deeds of the Faithful were truly an
abomination. It was reported that the sect assembled
at a secret meeting place every night; extinguishing
the candles, they would lie with each other's wives.
Reb Gedaliya was said to have secreted a whore sent
him by the sect in Zamość somewhere in his house

without the knowledge of his wife, Rechele. A copper cross hung on his breast, under the fringed vest, and an image lay in his breast pocket. At night Lilith and her attendants Namah and Machlot visited him, and they consorted together. Sabbath eve, dressing in scarlet garments and a fez, like a Muslim, he accompanied his disciples to the ruins of the old castle near Goray. There Samael presented himself to them, and they all prostrated themselves together before a clay image. Then they danced in a ring with torches in their hands. Rabbi Joseph de la Reina, the traitor, descended from Mount Seir to join them in the shape of a black dog. Afterward, as the legend went, they would enter the castle vaults and feast on flesh from the living—rending live fowl with their hands, and devouring the meat with the blood. When they had finished feasting, fathers would know their daughters, brothers their sisters, sons their mothers. Nechele, Levi's wife, strolled about unclothed, consorted with a coachman before the eyes of all the company—and of her own husband too. . . .

Goray became a den of robbers, an accursed town. The old residents were afraid to leave their homes, for children, who were also numbered among the Faithful, threw stones at the rival group. The children were particularly spiteful. They placed nails on the prayer-house seats of the old residents, causing them to tear their clothing; they cut the fringes of their prayer shawls, and molested their goats. Some boys even poured a bucket of slop down the chimney of a house and contaminated the vessels and food. The Faithful went so far as to write the government, charging their opponents with disloyalty, and they spilled oil on their goods; they even avenged themselves on small children. A woman who was returning from the bathhouse was ambushed in a back street by some hoodlums who attempted to rape her. She screamed and they ran away.

God's name was everywhere desecrated. In the villages the peasants already complained that the Jews had betrayed their faith and were behaving exactly like gypsies and outlaws. The priests were inciting the masses to a holy war. They foresaw all devout Christians gathering together, sword and spear in hand, to exterminate the Jews, man, woman, and child, so that not a trace should be left of the people of Israel (God save us!).

❦ 11 ❦

The Sacred and the Profane

Ever since Rechele had heard that Sabbatai Zevi had
donned the fez, the holy angels had ceased appearing
before her. She lay in her canopy bed long hours
every night, reciting holy names and awaiting a vision. She invoked cherubim and seraphim, meditated
on Metatron, the Lord of the Face, and petitioned
him until her lips grew weary and her strength
lapsed. But there was no reply. Just recently Bathsheba and Abigail would visit her and they would
study the mysteries together. When she was half-
asleep, Joseph the Righteous would appear in all his

beauty and grace and lead her through the heavenly mansions. He showed her the Garden of Eden and the Gates of Gehenna, the Treasures of Snow, and the Three Hundred and Ten Worlds to be inherited by the pious. When she awoke her legs would ache from so much climbing about in the celestial spheres. But now her thoughts were barren. In her sorrow she could not touch the morsels of honey cake that Chinkele set before her, or taste the sweet wine or other delicacies. She did not wash her hands, or recite the blessing over food, or pray, though she yearned for prayer. Her body, which had long ago lost its heat, would break out intermittently in perspiration. The hair sprouting on her shaven head pricked and hurt, her cheeks were hollow, her eyes dilated and her eyelids puffed. For the last few days her palate had been constantly dry, her tongue felt odd—it seemed entirely to fill her mouth; her teeth were set on edge as though she had eaten something sour; her legs were stiff and cumbersome. As though blown up with wind, her belly was distended.

At the beginning Reb Gedaliya tried to reason with Rechele and solace her. He explained that she had fallen from a high rung only to climb above it; he attempted to strengthen her with his words and to raise her spirits. Borrowing a fiddle, he played a Sabbath night melody for her in the middle of the week. He dispatched a messenger to buy her a necklace and bracelet, and invited the young wives to enter her room without asking permission and entertain her with merriment. He even sent Levi to Rechele to clarify the new ways of serving God and explicate the verse: "And I shall dwell with you in the midst of your uncleanliness." But Rechele greeted Levi with unrecognizing eyes, and was inattentive. Her soul seemed to be elsewhere.

Rechele experienced mysterious and terrifying things. Though her room was heated twice a day, she suffered constantly from cold chills that seemed to her to emanate within. Often her heart palpitated like a living creature; something contracted, coiled, and twisted like an imbedded snake in the recesses of her being. Her arms and legs were feeble, and loose in their joints. Her head hung down weakly, and she could not raise it. With nightfall she collapsed on her bed, where she remained in a trance for several hours. Her skull seemed to be filled with sand, her mouth was agape. She always woke at the same moment, in a panic, as though deathbed watchers had brought her back to life with their screams. Her throat was narrow and swollen, almost strangled; her congealed blood slowly warmed and began to flow again through her veins. It would seem to Rechele that her body had actually died and gradually was reviving.

But what had happened to Rechele the prophetess? Piety and the grace of God had left her. She had lost all inclination to study the holy books, and lacked interest in worldly affairs. She received visitors coldly, and confused their names. She had ceased to bathe every morning and no longer wore her finery. For a long time now someone inside her had been thinking twistedly, someone had been asking questions, and replying—as though a dialogue went on in her mind, complicated, tedious, with neither start nor conclusion. For days and nights on end the argument extended. Lofty words were spoken, the Torah was explained meticulously, as well as secular works; the disputants were obdurate. Often Rechele tried to comprehend the grounds of the dispute and later to recall them; but they were elusive, like words in a dream. Sometimes it seemed to Rechele that these things were only occurring within her; at other moments she saw visions that appeared and disappeared in an instant, leaving her uncertain as to what had actually happened. Once Rechele distinguished one of the disputants crying:

"God has died! The Husk shall reign for ever and ever!"

It was a tall man who said this, ash-gray, terrifying, cobwebby. Long strands of hair hung from his head; an evil, mocking smile swept across his pitted, discolored countenance. Soon after he had spoken, another voice chanted the verse from the Passover Haggadah:

"I am the Lord! I am He, and no other!"

The sacred and the profane were engaged in a disputation. The sacred had a face, but no body. The Face was flushed, as after the bath, had a white beard and long, blown earlocks. A velvet skull cap sat on its high forehead. The Face swayed in prayer; it spoke with zeal, like Rabbi Benish in the old days, chanting the holy writ; it raised questions of Torah and resolved them; it told pious tales to strengthen the faith and vanquish disbelief. With sacred pride, the Face recited the blessing before meals, and prayers that come at the beginning and the end of the Sabbath, as well as whole sections from the liturgy and the Zohar. Sometimes shutting her eyes, Rechele could see the Face surging up from the darkness. Tiny old-man's wrinkles quivered in the corners of its eyes. Delicate blue veins shone in its red cheeks, its eyes smiled with grandfatherly grace.

The Profane was situated in some distant place, in darkness, deep down, like a cellar. Sometimes he spoke very low, voicelessly. Hidden and veiled, he lay inside some web or cocoon. Often, he changed shape —at times he looked human, at other times like a bat or a spider. At moments all that Rechele could see was an open mouth, askew like a frog's. The Profane was audacious, making lewd remarks. Then his voice boomed from the pit, or the cave, where he lay concealed. Taunting and blaspheming, he bandied about the names of holy men and angels. A stream of vulgarities escaped his lips. He jested and mocked profusely, bringing Rechele to the verge of laughter, though she knew that to be sinful.

Where did such shameful thoughts come from? The Profane called the nether parts of men and women by their crudest names; he showed Rechele vile sights, and discovered obscene meanings in Biblical verses.

Nor did he spare the patriarchs and King David,
Bathsheba and Queen Esther. He depicted the copu-
lation of beasts and animals, an ox with a woman, and
a man with a sow. He told tales of women who lay at
night with monstrous men, and of girls who had as-
signations with goblins and evil spirits. He recited
magical incantations in Aramaic, and invoked destroyer demons in Latin. Sometimes the Profane
would begin to babble in a strange tongue, cackling
toothlessly and throatily, as though something tickled
him. At other times he poked fun at Rechele in
rhyme:

> *Rechele, now*
> *I'll teach thee how.* . . .

Rechele was terrified of the Profane, for he grew
stronger from day to day, entangling her. Sometimes,
when Rechele lay down and shut her eyes, the Face
of the sacred would begin to recede until, becoming
as small as a nut, it would disappear. One night Rechele found herself in a fenced-in place, full of
mounds, and thorns, and stones—like a cemetery. In
the dubious dusk, broken pots and rags lay about;
there were puddles of water, as though a corpse had
been washed here. She stood before a hut with no
opening except for a round hole in the wall, whence
steam issued. A dying light seeped through the cracks
of the hut, and some lunglike, red, and swollen thing
peered out. Afraid, Rechele wanted to run away, but
her legs were leaden and faltering. Desperately she

tried to run, but in her helplessness only became lost
in some subterranean passage with bolted shutters,
blind walls, and crooked rafters. Rechele clambered
up hill and down, wormed through small openings;
with feeble arms she climbed wavering ladders and
pulled herself up ropes. But she continued to sink,
and the lower she sank the darker it became, the more
suffocating the air. A bearded figure pursued her,
hairy and naked, wet and stinking, with long monkey
hands and open maw. Catching her at last, he carried her as light as a feather (for she had all at once
become weightless) and flew with her over dusk-
filled streets and tall buildings, through a skyless
space full of mounds, and pits, and pollution. At their
back ran hosts of airy things, half-devil and half-man,
pointing at them, pursuing them. The Thing swept
her over steep rooftops, gutters, and chimneys, huge
and mildewy; there was no escape. It was stifling and
the Thing pressed her to him, leaned against her.
The Thing was a male; he wanted to ravish her. He
squeezed her breasts; he tried to force her legs apart
with his bony knees. He spoke to her rapidly,
hoarsely, breathing hard, imploring and demanding:
"Rechele! Quick! Let me! I want to defile you!"
"No, no!"
"Rechele, make a covenant with me!"
"No, no!"
"Rechele, you are already defiled!"
He threw her down, and entered her. She cried a
bitter cry, but there was no sound, and she started

from sleep. With perfect clarity she saw that the dark house was crowded with evil things, insane beings running hither and thither, hopping as on hot coals, quivering and swaying, as though they were all kneading a great trough of dough. A mocking exultation shone in their faces. Rechele could not remember who she was, where she was, or what had happened. Her head was weighted like stone, her skin covered with a glutinous substance. At times Reb Gedaliya heard her gasping. With a candle, he hurried to her bedside. He rubbed her temples with vinegar, blew on her and fanned her, to drive away the intruder. Reb Gedaliya spat three times, and searched every corner of the room for some sign of the visitations. His large hands trembled; perspiration dripped from his body to Rechele's featherbed, and he shouted as though she were hard of hearing:

"Wake up! Rechele! Don't be afraid! Thou hast seen a goodly vision! A goodly vision hast thou seen! Goodly is the vision thou hast seen!"

❦ 12 ❦

Rechele Is Impregnated by Satan

There was famine in Goray. In the half-empty shops shopkeepers dozed before cold stoves; for lack of tools artisans were idle; everything had crumbled that summer. Hollow stalks had been reaped in the fields, and there was no seed for sowing. Abandoning their families, peasants begged throughout the countryside; their emaciated horses were driven from the stalls to become prey to wolves. So devastating a famine had not been known for many years. People were found frozen on the roads; the mills stood motionless, for there was no grain to mill.

The people of Goray were debilitated. Heavy persons turned saffron-yellow, began to limp, and a white film like perspiration covered their eyeballs. Slender persons developed the shiny, puffed faces associated with toothache. Chatterboxes became silent, pranksters ceased their jokes. Even the children forgot to be mischievous, and anxiety stared from their eyes as from those of the old. From early morning till late at night the men sat in the study house, warming themselves before the broad clay oven. In the beginning they still disputed. The Faithful said that Sabbatai Zevi reigned in Stamboul and that he had sent messengers to the Ten Tribes urging them to join him and to disregard what he had done, for his deeds had been decreed in Heaven. The first fifty ships loaded with mighty warriors, chariots, and arms had already embarked, in preparation for battle. But the Opponents were certain that Sabbatai Zevi, who had changed his name to Muhammed Bashi, had become a caliph and a Jew-hater, and had been responsible for an expulsion of pious Jews. Often the disputants came to blows, tore letters and pamphlets to shreds, wielded belts and drew blood.

But now, as though nothing more could be said, there was silence. Despair gripped the town. The old men publicly deloused themselves and snored without restraint on the study house tables and benches. Boys played at Goat and Wolf and never looked into books, since no one cared what they did. There was no longer even sinning; the Evil Spirit himself

seemed to have dozed off; every man went his solitary
way. The occasional itinerant who found himself in
Goray walked the streets disconsolately for a while,
and then, with empty bag and a curse on his lips, departed.

Alas for Goray—every visitation fell upon it! Despite the winter, fires were frequent. Houses seemed
to catch fire by themselves, and burned to the ground.
Only pot shards and bare chimneys remained. More
than ever, this year, people slipped, breaking arms
and legs. Because the barns were empty, field mice
entered the houses. Polecats strangled chickens, and
even bit children. Thieves broke into the homes of
those who lived on the environs of town; bears and
boars lurked on the roads. The destroyer demons had
been reveling freely in the streets of Goray. Every
night they beat on the windowpanes of Reb Godel
Chasid's house. When a candle was lit, the shadow of
a bony hand with five outspread fingers could be distinguished on the wall opposite. Groaning, as of a
woman in labor, issued from the chimney of Levi's
house. On Thursday imps overturned the dough
troughs, spilling the dough for the white Sabbath
bread; they threw handfuls of salt into the pots where
dinner was being cooked, ripped the *mezuzot* from
door posts, and held weddings in desolate places.
Imps would hang on to the wheelspokes of a wagon,
dragging the wagon back and blinding the horse.
Disguising themselves as he-goats, they danced to
meet the women returning from the bathhouse. Late

one afternoon when Chinkele was on her way to prayers in the women's section, she saw a black-skinned beast crawling at her in the light of the rising moon. She tried to run, but the monstrosity reared up on its hind legs, like a man, and pursued her until she fell into a ditch. The next evening the same creature scared some children in the street. One of the boys heard the beast shout something in a gentile tongue. Everyone immediately understood that this was a werewolf. Some whispered that it was the mad lord Zamoyski, for once the werewolf fired a pistol and threw down some gold ducats. They ran off to tell Reb Gedaliya and Rechele the Prophetess about this—but there, also, evil reigned.

Rechele had been impregnated by Satan. She confessed this herself to her husband: Samael had come to her at night, and had violated her. A destroyer demon grew in her womb. She bade Reb Gedaliya probe her belly, and he discovered that, indeed, it was tight as a drum. Rechele also told Reb Gedaliya that she no longer menstruated, and she showed him where the demons had made seven braids in her hair. At first Reb Gedaliya would not believe Rechele, and maintained that she imagined it all. At night he would kindle many lights in her room, place amulets everywhere, and recite various adjurations, for he wished to remain with Rechele. But the moment he lay at her side all the candles were extinguished, and he received a blow on the temples that flung him out of bed. Then he would hear a voice cry:

"Touch her not, for she has made a covenant with me! Arise and go quickly!"

From then on Reb Gedaliya avoided all intercourse with Rechele and left her alone. He even drove Chinkele away and took instead a mute servant girl, to keep people from discovering this latest disgrace. Because his beloved wife had been stolen from him, Reb Gedaliya began to drink and slept all day on his bench bed. His friends fell away from him, and he would certainly have been driven out of town if the butchers had not sided with him. Meanwhile, horrifying things happened to Rechele.

Every night Satan visited Rechele to torment her. He was black and tall, fiery-eyed and with a long tail; his body was cold, his lips scaly, and he exhaled pitchfire. He ravished her so many times that she was powerless to move. Then, rising, he tormented her in numerous ways. Pulling the hairs singly from her head, he wound them about her throat; he pinched her in the hips and bit her breasts with his jagged teeth. When she yawned he spat down her throat; he poured water on her bedsheet and pretended she had wet her bed. He made her show him her private parts and drink slop. He seduced her into reciting the explicit name of God and blaspheming Him; on Friday nights he forced her to desecrate the Sabbath by tearing paper and touching the Sabbath candlesticks. Sometimes Satan told Rechele obscene tales, and Reb Gedaliya on the other side of the wall would hear her loud, mad laughter resounding at midnight. Once,

Reb Gedaliya opened the door of the Holy Ark to take out the Torah scroll, only to find the scroll mantle slashed, and a piece of dung lying within. . . .

Rechele suffered extraordinary tortures. At times the evil one blew up one of her breasts. One foot swelled. Her neck became stiff. Rechele extracted little stones, hairs, rags, and worms from wet, pussy abscesses formed on the flesh of her thigh and under her arms. Though she had long since stopped eating, Rechele vomited frequently, venting reptiles that slithered out tail first. At times she barked like a dog, lowed like a cow, neighed like a horse, or made sounds of the lion and the leopard. There were days when she could not open her mouth; and there were others when she was deaf. Occasionally, she would squint and become cross-eyed, and her tongue would stammer incomprehensibly, as though she spoke in her sleep. The pills she was given for her illness remained in her throat, and she had to spit them out again.

Rechele's name had become a byword. Reb Gedaliya struggled vainly to conceal what had happened, for the walls have ears. Her odd behavior was remarked on everywhere. At night when the moon shone, Rechele went into the snow, barefoot and in her nightgown. Sleepwalking, she visited the cemetery, where she crawled among the tombstones; scratching in the dirt with her fingernails, she unburied dead infants, and she climbed up on the apex of sepulchers. She had been observed sitting at the rim of a well and crowing like a rooster. One woman swore she had seen Rechele riding on a broom, with a dog rolling after her on a hoop.

The village runners encountered Rechele sitting on the banks of the river rinsing clothing. The tale of what had happened to Rechele spread to Yanov, Turbin, Zamosć, Krasnik, and even to Lublin, for her name was famous in all these places as that of a prophetess. The peasants, also, knew that Satan had entered into the body of a daughter of the Jews, and this visitation was spoken of at fairs and in taverns. The shutters of Reb Gedaliya's house were bolted day and night, and he did not show his face outdoors until dusk fell. Then Reb Gedaliya would wrap himself in his great coat and set out for the slaughterhouse, carrying a heavy stick and a lantern, afraid of people and the mockery in their glances.

🦋 13 🦋

The Dybbuk *of Goray*

A marvellous tale treating of a woman that was possessed of a dybbuk (God preserve us): Taken from the worthy book The Works of the Earth and rendered into Yiddish to the end that women and girls and common folk might perfectly comprehend the wonder of it all and that they might set their hearts on returning to God's ways: And that they might be instructed in how great is the punishment of the sinner who staineth his soul (God save us): May the Al-

*mighty protect us from all evil and avert his
wrath from us and expel Satan and his like
for ever and ever Amen:*

AND IT CAME TO PASS in the town of Goray that lay
among the hills near the holy communities of Zamość, Turbin, Krashnik *et al.* where formerly dwelt
the author of the work *Holy Offering* and where lat-
terly Rabbi Benish Ashkenazy occupied the rabbinic
chair (the remembrance of the righteous be a blessing to us all). It happened in that terrible year when
the pillars of the earth trembled with the deed of
Sabbatai Zevi (may the memory of him be blotted
out): Who (for our sins are great) was himself converted and did seduce many others from the paths of
righteousness and many pious amongst them and he
lighted a fire in every corner of the Exile: May God
who is a jealous and an avenging God give him his
due and repay the wicked for his wickedness as he de-
serveth and may we all be deemed worthy to witness
a true and a full redemption speedily and in our days
and let us say Amen:

AND IN THE TOWN of Goray there dwelt a man
renowned far and wide for he was a Godfearing man
and had a pleasing countenance and his deeds were
good and the name of this man was Gedaliya: And
this man was versed in the uses of the cabala and in
the mysteries: To wit he could draw wine from a wall
and was expert in the science of alchemy and every
Sabbath eve he created a third-born calf like unto the

tradition concerning our holy Amoraim: This man
also knew many nostrums for he was a sage and he
found favor in the eyes of all men with his understanding and smooth tongue: But in fact he was a son
of Belial and entirely wicked and all that he did he
did to provoke the blessed Creator: For in secret he
invoked the name of the profane and he con-
jured up Lilith Naamah Machlot and all the other
destroyer demons that they might do his will and that
he might do their will: And after this fashion he
amassed treasures of gold, silver, diamonds and precious stones: And he deceived the townspeople and
knew their wives and fathered bastards without number: And in his lust and license he did shameful
things such as are not proper to be written in a book
and a word to the wise should be sufficient:

AND LO (for his sins that were many) his own wife
too (whom he had cunningly stolen from her husband
a most righteous man) fell prisoner in the net of the
Outer Ones and a *dybbuk* possessed her: And for that
she had the name of a righteous woman and Elijah
revealed himself to her; no son of man could rightly
believe the tidings that came to his ears and all were
curious to ascertain whether or no there was truth in
the report: And there was: For the young woman
(Rechele was her name) lay naked in her house and
her shame was uncovered and all the utensils were
broken and the bed linen was torn and she cried a
loud and a bitter cry: And when all the elders of the
town and its leaders gathered together they could not

recognize her: For her shape was completely changed and her face was as chalk and her lips were twisted as with a seizure (God save us) and the pupils of her eyes were turned back after an unnatural fashion: And the voice that cried from her was not her voice: For her voice was a woman's voice and the *dybbuk* cried with the voice of a man with such weeping and wailing that terror seized all that were there and their hearts dissolved with fear and their knees trembled: And for that she lay with parted legs like a woman in labor on the stool the women desired to put her legs together for it was a shame before the men and they also did cover her: But at once her garments fell from her body for the evil spirit cast them off: And the strength in her limbs was unnaturally great so that even the men could not prevail and the thing was a marvel to all and a mystery indeed:

AND IT CAME TO PASS that when Reb Gedaliya saw what had transpired and what had occurred to him that he was greatly ashamed and shame did cover his face: For he thought in his heart, What will people say: If the spirit has taken possession of Reb Gedaliya's wife and he has discovered no counsel to prevent it then surely he is no righteous man and all his amulets are false and people would mock him and revenge themselves upon him: And therefore in his cunning he said, You see now she is out of her mind and all her words are the words of a madwoman: Then the *dybbuk* began to scream: Alas and alack to

thee thou wicked man Thou hast worked unrighteous-
ness and thou hast polluted thy soul with every un-
worthy thing and thou hast lain with whores and thou
hast fornicated: And thinkest thou now to deny the
sight of thine own eyes lest that thy wickedness become known to men and that thou mightest further
beguile them with thy cunning and with thy inso-
lence: And it came to pass that when Reb Gedaliya
heard these words the strength ebbed from his body:
But anon he revived and cried, She is mad completely: But the people would hear him no longer and
they would not believe him: And there was a pious
man, one Reb Mordecai Joseph (may his remembrance be a blessing to us all) who formerly had
descended to the nethermost Sheol and afterward
had done penance and had saved his soul: And he
was zealous for the zeal of God and he lifted up his
stick and he smote Gedaliya: And he cried, Thou
wretched man now shalt thou blind the eyes of this
people no longer: For thou art a seducer and a magician and thou art the cause that the plague has been
poured out on us all and that we must drink the cup
of persecution to the dregs: Then the mighty Gedaliya would have killed him but the people took his
part and defended him:

AND NOW did the *dybbuk* scream ever more loudly
and he confessed his sins with a fearful lamentation
and groaning: And the woman lifted a heavy stone
and smote her breast: And the marvel was that her
limbs were not broken nor her frame shattered for

so heavy was the stone that three strong men could
not move it from its place: But in her hands it was as
a feather: And she smote her body with the stone
from the top of her head to the tips of her toes time
and again without interruption: And that pious man
Reb Mordecai Joseph (his remembrance be a blessing unto us) girded his loins and asked, Why dost
thou scream and bring her so much woe:

AND THE DYBBUK replied in a loud and piercing
voice: How then shall I not cry and how then shall I
not wail: Seeing that when I walked among the living I polluted my soul and transgressed every transgression cited in the Torah: I hail from Lublin and
there I was one of those frivolous youths that swill
beer in the taverns and frolic in the whore houses:
And I rebelled at every command of God and in-
curred His wrath: On the holy Sabbath day I did
work and I did eat of the pig and of the other forbidden foods: And on Yom Kippur I made a feast for
spite and drank wine and gave myself to unbridled
desire and I also lay with beasts, animals and fowls:
Woe is me for I said in my heart, There is neither
Justice nor Judge, and I denied that the Torah is
from Heaven and I despised all wise scholars and I
brazenly swore at them and I set dogs on them as is
the practice of pranksters: When lo suddenly I suffered a stroke and this is a sickness that no one ever
rises from: And I saw clearly that my end was come:
But (such is the way of the wicked) I grew not sub-
missive and I remained haughty at the very gate of

Gehenna and before my death my comrades came to me and they asked me Abraham (such was my name) dost thou repent: And I answered them in my pride, Now even now I do not believe that there is a Creator in the world and before I expired I blasphemed and thus my soul left me denying Him:

AND IT CAME TO PASS that I had but died and had not yet been lifted up and laid in the earth that three evil spirits seized me: And they tormented me cruelly and they trampled on me with their feet and they sorely afflicted me: And then I saw that indeed there is a punishment only it was already too late: And all the time I lay covered they perpetrated on me all manner of suffering that cannot be recounted: And I called on my kin that they might discover me some relief but they could not hear my voice for I was already not of this world: And tens of thousands and millions of milliards of imps followed my funeral: And they were all my children that I had created through continual defilement and fornication: And they called me Father and my shame was boundless:

AND WHEN they had laid me in the grave and piled the last shovelful of earth upon me there came to me the Angel Dumah: And he rapped on my grave with his fiery rod and the grave split open at once: And he called *Mah Shemecha* (What is thy name) and I could not remember the verse for I had not prayed: And the angel cried Thou foul seed Thou sinner against the Lord of Israel Tarry not here and abandon this grave and fly away to the hollow of the sling: For

thy place is not in the graveyard where so many
righteous and proper men rest in peace: And I tried
to implore him but he tore the shrouds from my
body and he beat me with his fiery rod and he drove
me out:

AND LO without there lay in wait for me vast armies
of demons and destroyer spirits and messengers of
annihilation and they were all in readiness to fling
themselves at me in their wrath and to rend me to
bits: And they came at me in anger and mockery and
they gave chase to me and they whistled and howled
and pursued me through the wilderness: I sought to
flee them and to escape them but there was no hiding
place and they captured me and they cast me and
tossed me like a bird in the wind: One pulled me
from the right hand and one from the left and they
would not let me be by day or by night and they delighted in my terror: Oh were all the heavens parchment and all the seas ink would they not yet suffice
to inscribe one thousandth part of my ordeal: In
my anguish I passed into the leaf of a tree: But there
too my sorrow was immeasurable for when the leaf
shook in the wind I shivered and twisted exactly as
though I were a living man: Yet so long as I dwelt in
the leaf the demons could do me no evil: But I was
forced to leave it for a worm crept into the leaf and
it bit me: And the instant I left the leaf the black
hosts ringed me wildly about and they rolled me
through every wilderness and desert and wasteland
full of serpents and scorpions and horned snakes:

And in my straits I entered into a frog: But there too things were bitter for me, for a man cannot dwell in a frog that breeds in the swamp and in stinking marshes: Also the frog suffered and sickened and her belly swelled: And thus I passed from creature to creature: Moreover for many years I dwelt in a millstone and when it turned it rubbed against my limbs and my pain knew no bounds:

AND REB MORDECAI JOSEPH asked the *dybbuk* How didst thou enter into the woman and by what means didst thou gain the ascendancy over her: And the *dybbuk* said Let it be known that Gedaliya is a denier of the faith and an apostate out of spite and that he has defiled his wife with many defilements and hence I was able to gain the ascendancy over her: For one morning the woman desired to start a fire with two flint stones and the sparks would not light the wick: And she cried out the name of Satan: And the moment I heard this I entered into her body:

AND REB MORDECAI JOSEPH said to the spirit, Through what opening didst thou force thy way into the woman, and the *dybbuk* spoke and said Through *that same place:*

THEN REB MORDECAI JOSEPH rose and smote Gedaliya with violence: Moreover the other men flung themselves at him and beat him and shed his blood and tore his beard until he fell fainting to the ground: And Reb Mordecai Joseph (may his remembrance be a blessing) flogged him forty times forty until his blood flowed like water: And the people took him and flung him into the jail that is in the prayer house anteroom. And they chained him to the post and there he remained to await his judgment: For the gentiles too were sentencing witches in their judgments and many of them were burned at the stake: And they appointed a watchman to watch him:

🐾 14 🐾

The Death of Rechele

AND IT CAME TO PASS after these things when the
wicked Gedaliya had been imprisoned that Reb Mordecai Joseph (may his remembrance be a blessing)
bade powerful men carry the young woman to the
study house where the evil spirit might be driven out
of her: For the *dybbuk* did weary her with all manner
of torment and caused the name of God to be desecrated (God preserve us) and there was great sym-
pathy for the woman: And the powerful men rose
and took the woman in their arms and against her
will and bore her off to the court of the prayer

house: All this time the woman was still and silent as though her strength had deserted her and she was like a little child: But when they came near to the door of the prayer house anteroom then did the *dybbuk* begin to scream and wail, Bring me not nearer to this place For I cannot endure the holy air, and the sound of his outcry was heard far and wide: But the men did not heed the *dybbuk* and they carried the woman into the study house by main force though she wrestled with them: And she worked with a strength exceeding the strength of a man for her power came from the evil spirit (*vid. sup.*):

AND IT CAME ABOUT that when the woman lay on the pulpit the *dybbuk* burst into a weeping such that all who heard wept with him: For not women alone but men as well were overcome with compassion: And the *dybbuk* cried and said: Why have ye no pity on me and why do ye work all this to vex me and to distress me: Seeing that ye know full well that every thing that is holy causes me much suffering and may be compared to a needle in the flesh of a living man: Now search ye out and discover What injustice hath been done unto this woman through me: Who before I entered into her was weak and sickly and she required broth for her nourishment and she was compelled to lean on a stick for support: And now behold for that I have entered into her she has grown powerful and is able to lift up heavy burdens and go into the cold without warm garments and do all that her heart desires: Therefore what is the matter that ye

have all come together to undo me and particularly since I am of the seed of Israel and have great
fear of the Outer Ones: Who some of them have the
faces of boars with eight heads and the poison under
their snouts is all fire from the valley of the shadow of
death: And others of them butt with their horns ram-
like and they are called Hairy Goat Ones: And their
fur is covered with tar and the bristles thereof are of
thorns to affright the sinful, and their dwelling place
is beyond the Hills of Darkness: Now I implore ye,
Give me leave to dwell in her body and I swear Not
a hair of her head shall be harmed and I shall guard
her like the apple of my eye that no mishap may
trouble her: And when the allotted measure of my
suffering shall be full and I shall be given leave to
endure my judgment in Gehenna for the space of
twelve months why then I shall forsake the woman
with no further ado and unloose her and leave her
in peace:

AND THE SPIRIT spoke these words with cunning
purpose to deceive the people and to mock them:
And there were indeed some simple folk who in their
innocence believed the words of the *dybbuk* to be
true and they wished him to be spared: But the pious
Reb Mordecai Joseph (may his remembrance be a
blessing) comprehended the demon's wiles (for he
was a great cabalist) and he cried, No, Depart thou
from her and go forth to that place where no man
dwelleth and where no cattle of the field sets foot
For it is not seemly thou shouldst continue among the

living: And when Reb Mordecai Joseph had uttered
these words he meditated on such holy names and
formed such unions and made such combinations and
described such circles and rings as are within the ken
of those that are knowing in the mysteries:

THEN DID THE SPIRIT abandon gentle words and begin with the harsh words and a fire seethed from his
nostrils and he cried in a loud voice that made the
walls shake:

WHO ART THOU and of what merit is the house of
thy forebears that thou thinkest to contend with me:
Dost thou believe that thou art a master of His name
and wise in cabala: No, For thou art a complete ig-
noramus and thy combinations can never be effica-
cious: And the *dybbuk* spoke a saying in the vulgar
tongue *They shall avail as cupping avails the dead:*
And he cursed Reb Mordecai Joseph (may his remembrance be a blessing) and played tricks upon
him such as were never seen or heard since the world
began, and the multitude laughed at the pious Reb
Mordecai Joseph: And there was a great desecration
of God's name for the *dybbuk* uttered obscenities
and played the fool and there was hee-hawing and
guffawing: And first he reckoned up the secret sins of
each one and called them by name and winked with
his eyes and asked Dost thou not remember such and
such a place, and there arose a hubbub: For he put
the wives of respectable men to shame and revealed
that the rabbi's wife had played the whore, and he
published slander concerning many families and all

with contumely and effrontery: And (for that we have transgressed) no one dared give the *dybbuk* the lie and he grew bolder and discovered things that had lain hidden, giving clear signs of proof: He reminded one woman that she had a mole under her breast: Another that she had a birth mark, another a boil, another a scar, another lice, etc.: And he also repeated things that are betwixt *him* and *her,* man and wife: And then he frolicked, singing songs and all in rhyme so that all who heard were amazed, for it is not the practice for women to produce such inventions: And he derided the women and their habitudes: How they blessed the candles on Sabbaths and holidays and how they tithed the white bread and burned it and how they picked peas and their gesticulations in the bathhouse and in the prayer house: And he worked this all with malice that the women might be ugly in the eyes of their husbands: And he called the pious with bynames in the German tongue to wit *trop lekish parech esel shemosh pushkemeckler kaltoon bock, et al.* (pinhead loony scab ass slattern meddler stinkpot he-goat) and in the Polish tongue and in Ivan's tongue as well: And he sang the bridal canopy tunes with great skill *item* the Covering Tune for when the groom covers the bride's hair, *item* the Canopy Dance Tune, *item* the Escort Tune for when bride and groom are escorted to their chamber: And he mimicked the sound of the fife and of the cymbal and of the bagpipe and of the other instruments and all with locked lips and the hearts of the congregation were melted like wax at the sight of the woman's gesticulations and grimaces: And there were present flippant, light-headed persons that had never believed in transmogrification and now when they saw this with their own eyes they fell on their faces and beat their breasts and tore their garments and there was a great tumult:

THEN DID REB MORDECAI JOSEPH (may his remembrance be a blessing) collect his strength and he bade a censer be fetched and onycha and wax and incense and other spices and glowing coals: And he bade black candles be lighted and they brought the board of purification and he enveloped himself in a white robe and another ten men put on prayer shawls and phylacteries and the chanter took a ram's horn in his hand: And he opened the doors of the Holy Ark and he drew out thence a Torah scroll and he cried: Be quick and fly Or I shall excommunicate thee and drive thee off by force: And he laid all the spice on the censer and the smoke of the incense arose for it is notorious that the smell of incense undoes the Husk: *And thus it came to pass:*

FOR WHEN THE SPIRIT smelled the smoke of the holy incense he uttered a great and bitter cry and he sprang as high as the rafters, and the woman rolled on the floor and a foam dribbled from her mouth like an epileptic (God preserve us): And for spite the spirit flung her bonnet to the earth and uncovered her body, and she spread her legs to show her nakedness and to bring men into thoughts of transgression: And

she passed water and befouled the holy place and her
breasts became as hard as stones and her belly bulged
so that ten men could not depress it: Her left leg she
twisted around her neck and the right she stuck out
stiff as a board and her tongue lolled like a hanged
man's (God preserve us): In this state she lay and
her cries went up to very Heaven and the earth was
split by her cries: And she vomited blood and filth and
it dripped from her nostrils and from her eyes and she
broke wind: And many of the congregation turned
sick with revulsion: One time she laughed and one
time she cried and she sobbed and ground her teeth:
And many righteous women did testify that a stink
issued from *that same place* for the spirit dwelt in
there (*vid. sup.*): and she also made such lewd gesticulations as cannot be put down in writing: And when
they placed a holy object near her, to wit a page from
a discarded holy volume, or the thread of a prayer
shawl fringe, why she leaped up and flew through the
air: And all this to the accompaniment of thunder
and lightning, so that many of the congregation were
struck with terror and their knees knocked and they
cried: Woe unto us, For the profane doth triumph
over the sacred (which God forbid);

THEN DID REB MORDECAI JOSEPH (may his remembrance be a blessing) cry Blow the blast and he
who held the ram's horn blew: And Reb Mordecai
Joseph cried I excommunicate thee: May every curse
and every ban in the Chapter of Curses fall on thy
head if thou forsake not the body of this woman im-

mediately and out of hand: And the chanter chanted
the Chapter of Curses and sprinkled ashes on the
woman's head: And there was such a turbulence in
the study house that the gentiles came running up
too and their priest with them and they bowed for
they saw that this thing was from on high and they
prayed to their God: And some of them cried that the
woman be put to death for that she was a witch: And
the congregation stood so close in the prayer house
that no more could enter and there was a great press:

AND THE DYBBUK cried Make me free of the ban
and I undertake to leave in good faith for I can
withstand the sacred no longer: And Reb Mordecai
Joseph (may his remembrance be a blessing) did as
the *dybbuk* had bidden promising to study the Mishna
in his name and to recite the Mourner's Prayer after
his soul and he solaced the *dybbuk* and lifted the ban:
But at once the evil spirit denied himself and he
cried: No, Here it is better for me and I shall not
depart: Then Reb Mordecai Joseph laid him under a
ban again and threatened the *dybbuk* and adjured
him and this went on hour after hour for the *dybbuk*
did nought but lie and perjure himself with his
crooked tongue: And he boasted that the holy names
held no terror for him and he denied the blessed
God: And when they asked him Why then art thou
punished he replied It is all chance and an event of
nature: And thus he continued in his rebelliousness:
Oh if we were to undertake to tell but one thousandth
part of all that the fiend did and his ribaldry and his

lewdness this tongue would be too brief to recount it and this sheet to record it: But the whole congregation saw with perfect clearness the wonders of God and set their hearts on returning to their Father in Heaven: And the name of the Almighty was consecrated that day:

AND IT CAME TO PASS toward evening that the spirit cried Look after yourselves For I am about to forsake the body of this woman, seeing that the blasts of the ram's horn and the adjurations have left me no place here: And he began to weep with a man's tears and he said Pray that He show me compassion for I am in dire straits: And dusk fell on the study house for it was wintertime and the days were short: And the congregation all recited the verse beginning *And let there be contentment* and various psalms and other prayers to drive the spirit away: When suddenly the spirit cried: Move off for I come: And there was such a press for very terror that many folk were trampled: The next instant the congregation beheld a flash of fire from *that same place* and it flew through the window burning a round hole in the pane: And no man opened his mouth for all were struck dumb with shock:

BUT RECHELE LAY on the earth like dead for her strength had come from the spirit (*vid. sup.*): And the women hastened and covered her and they bore her to her house to revive her and to bring her back to life:

AND MANY NIGHTS thereafter the evil spirit visited

her and rapped on her window and spoke to her
sweetly: And he said, But see As long as I dwelt in
thee thou were in good health: And now art thou
sickly and poorly: But let me return to thy body and
remove the amulets from thy throat and I shall do
thy pleasure: And the spirit spoke in this manner
smooth words and pleasant but the woman would not
heed him: And then he warned her that she would
be repayed for this and that he would have his revenge: And so it came to pass (because of our transgressions that are great): For on the morning of the
third day when the women came to Rechele to tend
her they found her dead and her body was already
cold: And they did what was proper with her: And
Reb Itche Mates her first husband mourned her and
recited the Mourner's Prayer over her grave: And in
his love for her that knew no bounds he took the
thing to heart and he sickened: And before he died
he bade that he be buried near her: And thus that
righteous man passed away with a kiss: May his merit
be our shield:

AND THE WICKED GEDALIYA persuaded the watchman and the latter removed his chains and they fled
together: And Gedaliya became an apostate (God
save us) and rose to high position among the idolators
and a troubler of Jews: And some folk say that Gedaliya was none other than Samael himself and that all
his deeds were nought but seduction: And the moral
of this tale is:

LET NONE ATTEMPT TO FORCE THE LORD: TO END OUR
PAIN WITHIN THE WORLD: THE MESSIAH WILL COME
IN GOD'S OWN TIME: AND FREE MEN OF DESPAIR
AND CRIME: THEN DEATH WILL PUT AWAY
HIS SWORD: AND SATAN DIE ABJURED,
ABHORRED: LILITH WILL VANISH
WITH THE NIGHT: THE EXILE
END AND ALL BE LIGHT:
AMEN SELAH:

CONCLUDED AND DONE